Should Smoking Be Banned?

Hal Marcovitz

INCONTROVERSY

ReferencePoint Press®

San Diego, CA

ReferencePoint Press®

About the Author

A former journalist, Hal Marcovitz is the author of more than 150 books for young readers. His other titles in the In Controversy series include Should Juvenile Offenders Be Tried as Adults? and How Serious a Problem Is Drug Use in Sports?

Printed in the United States

For more information, contact:
ReferencePoint Press, Inc.
PO Box 27779
San Diego, CA 92198
www.ReferencePointPress.com

Picture Credits:
Cover: iStockphoto.com
AP Images: 48, 71
© Richard Baker/In Pictures/Corbis: 63
© Bettmann/Corbis: 13
© Farrell Grehan/Corbis: 22
© Sigrid Olsson/PhotoAlto/Corbis: 43
© Richard Hamilton Smith/Corbis: 77
© Lee Snider/Photo Images/Corbis: 35
Thinkstock/Photodisc: 7
© Dusan Vranic/AP/Corbis: 55
© Brant Ward/San Francisco Chronicle/Corbis: 28
© Bobby Yip/Reuters/Corbis: 66

LIBRARY OF CONGRESS CATALOGING-IN-PUBLICATION DATA

Marcovitz, Hal.
Should smoking be banned? / by Hal Marcovitz.
p. cm. -- (In controversy series)
Includes bibliographical references and index.
ISBN-13: 978-1-60152-462-1 (hardback)
ISBN-10: 1-60152-462-5 (hardback)
1. Smoking--United States--Juvenile literature. 2. Smoking--Law and legislation--United States--Juvenile literature. I. Title.
HV5760.M377 2013
362.29'65610973--dc23

2012011486

Contents

In 2008, as the US economy and economies worldwide were falling into the worst recession since the Great Depression, most Americans had difficulty comprehending the complexity, magnitude, and scope of what was happening. As is often the case with a complex, controversial issue such as this historic global economic recession, looking at the problem as a whole can be overwhelming and often does not lead to understanding. One way to better comprehend such a large issue or event is to break it into smaller parts. The intricacies of global economic recession may be difficult to understand, but one can gain insight by instead beginning with an individual contributing factor, such as the real estate market. When examined through a narrower lens, complex issues become clearer and easier to evaluate.

This is the idea behind ReferencePoint Press's *In Controversy* series. The series examines the complex, controversial issues of the day by breaking them into smaller pieces. Rather than looking at the stem cell research debate as a whole, a title would examine an important aspect of the debate such as *Is Stem Cell Research Necessary?* or *Is Embryonic Stem Cell Research Ethical?* By studying the central issues of the debate individually, researchers gain a more solid and focused understanding of the topic as a whole.

Each book in the series provides a clear, insightful discussion of the issues, integrating facts and a variety of contrasting opinions for a solid, balanced perspective. Personal accounts and direct quotes from academic and professional experts, advocacy groups, politicians, and others enhance the narrative. Sidebars add depth to the discussion by expanding on important ideas and events. For quick reference, a list of key facts concludes every chapter. Source notes, an annotated organizations list, bibliography, and index provide student researchers with additional tools for papers and class discussion.

The *In Controversy* series also challenges students to think critically about issues, to improve their problem-solving skills, and to sharpen their ability to form educated opinions. As President Barack Obama stated in a March 2009 speech, success in the twenty-first century will not be measurable merely by students' ability to "fill in a bubble on a test but whether they possess 21st century skills like problem-solving and critical thinking and entrepreneurship and creativity." Those who possess these skills will have a strong foundation for whatever lies ahead.

No one can know for certain what sort of world awaits today's students. What we can assume, however, is that those who are inquisitive about a wide range of issues; open-minded to divergent views; aware of bias and opinion; and able to reason, reflect, and reconsider will be best prepared for the future. As the international development organization Oxfam notes, "Today's young people will grow up to be the citizens of the future: but what that future holds for them is uncertain. We can be quite confident, however, that they will be faced with decisions about a wide range of issues on which people have differing, contradictory views. If they are to develop as global citizens all young people should have the opportunity to engage with these controversial issues."

In Controversy helps today's students better prepare for tomorrow. An understanding of the complex issues that drive our world and the ability to think critically about them are essential components of contributing, competing, and succeeding in the twenty-first century.

After several weeks of debate, the New York City Council passed a new measure in 2011 that severely limits where smokers can enjoy their cigarettes. In past years the council had banned smoking in restaurants, bars, government buildings, and similar places. The new action took prohibitions against smoking a significant step further. Under the new legislation, people are no longer permitted to smoke in the city's 1,700 parks, 14 miles (22.5km) of city-owned beaches, and other public places, including the pedestrian mall in New York's famed Times Square. In other words, the council had banned smoking in all city-owned outdoor venues. "New Yorkers who go to our parks and beaches for some fresh air and fun will be able to breathe even cleaner air and sit on a beach not littered with cigarette butts,"[1] says Mayor Michael Bloomberg, who signed the measure into law. If caught smoking in the newly prohibited areas, smokers face fines of $50.

"New York City has been a leader on smoke-free issues and a lot of other cities will follow. What happens in New York tends to spread around the world."[2]

— Bronson Frick, associate director of the California-based Americans for Nonsmokers' Rights.

The action by the New York mayor and city council was welcomed by antismoking advocates in the city and elsewhere. Bronson Frick, associate director of the California-based Americans for Nonsmokers' Rights, says he hopes other cities follow New York's example and similarly ban smoking in their own parks. "New York City has been a leader on smoke-free issues and a lot of other cities will follow," Frick predicts. "What happens in New York tends to spread around the world."[2]

Mountain of Laws

It is likely that other American communities will meet Frick's expectations and find new ways to limit smoking. In the decades since 1964, when then US surgeon general Luther Terry issued his landmark report identifying cigarette smoking as a significant health hazard, federal, state, and local governments have adopted a mountain of laws regulating the sale and use of tobacco. Smokers once enjoyed the right to light up virtually anywhere they felt the craving—in restaurants, taverns, theaters, and even aboard buses, trains, and airplanes. Over the years, governments have enacted bans greatly limiting smoking indoors; the 2011 measure in New York City goes beyond that regulatory plateau, mandating where people can smoke outdoors.

Across the country, state and municipal governments have adopted bans on indoor smoking mainly because abundant medical

New York City's Central Park (pictured) is just one of the many city-owned public venues where smoking is no longer permitted. States and municipalities across the country have adopted measures banning indoor smoking, but only a few have banned outdoor smoking in public places.

evidence shows secondhand smoke is hazardous to people's health. Therefore, the laws specify, nonsmokers should not be forced to inhale the smoke from somebody else's cigarette that pollutes the air of an enclosed room. New York's prohibition on outdoor smoking runs counter to the long-held belief that secondhand smoke poses no threat to nonsmokers in an outdoor environment—that air currents carry the smoke away, making it unlikely that deadly chemicals found in tobacco smoke would enter the lungs of nonsmokers.

However, recent medical studies have found some evidence suggesting that secondhand smoke is a hazard wherever it may be exhaled. In 2010 Surgeon General Regina Benjamin declared in a report, "Even brief exposure to secondhand smoke can cause cardiovascular disease and could trigger acute cardiac events, such as heart attack. . . . Inhaling even the smallest amount of tobacco smoke can also damage your DNA, which can lead to cancer."[3]

The surgeon general's statement prompted council members in New York to act. "[Nonsmokers'] health and lives should not be negatively impacted because other people have decided to smoke,"[4] says council speaker Christine C. Quinn.

Inconclusive Science

There may have been enthusiasm on New York's City Council for banning smoking in outdoor places, but the vote was not unanimous. Twelve members of the 48-member council voted against the measure. Several council members believe the ban on outdoor smoking intrudes too far into people's rights. Council member Robert Jackson, who does not smoke, says, "We're moving towards a totalitarian society if in fact we're going to have those kinds of restrictions on New Yorkers."[5] And council member Daniel Halloran III says, "Once we pass this, we will next be banning smoking on sidewalks, and then in the cars of people who are driving minors and then in the homes."[6]

Other opponents question Benjamin's findings, arguing that the science is inconclusive on the hazards of being near a smoker outdoors. Says Michael B. Siegel, a professor of community health science at Boston University:

> In trying to convince people that even transient exposure to secondhand smoke is a potentially deadly hazard, smoking opponents risk losing scientific credibility. The anti-smoking movement has always fought with science on its side, but New York's ban on outdoor smoking seems to fulfill its opponents' charge that the movement is being driven instead by an unthinkable hatred of tobacco smoke.[7]

Limiting Access to Tobacco

Nevertheless, antismoking activists point out that strategies employed by New York City as well as by New York State have shown results. The city banned smoking in bars and restaurants in 2002. Meanwhile, the state taxes paid by New Yorkers who buy cigarettes by the pack or carton are the highest in the nation. Antismoking activists believe these measures have led to a smoking rate among New Yorkers that is below the national average. According to the Centers for Disease Control and Prevention (CDC), 15.8 percent of adults in New York City smoke, whereas the national average is 20.6 percent. "New York's numbers are below the national average because New York has implemented a comprehensive and aggressive approach that includes high taxes and hard-hitting anti-smoking campaigns,"[8] says Vince Wilmore, vice president of the Washington, DC–based advocacy group Campaign for Tobacco-Free Kids.

"In trying to convince people that even transient exposure to secondhand smoke is a potentially deadly hazard, smoking opponents risk losing scientific credibility."[7]

— Michael B. Siegel, professor of community health science at Boston University.

Given the impact of smoking on human health, it is likely that smokers and activists who support smokers' rights are likely to find further erosion in the number of places where smoking is permitted. Moreover, the federal government as well as many state and local lawmakers hope to make smoking more expensive by raising taxes on cigarettes. They also hope to further limit access to tobacco products to help dissuade young people from picking up the smoking habit. Smoking may never be completely banned, but for many people who enjoy cigarettes, it may well seem that it will be.

Facts

- According to a 2011 report by the office of New York City mayor Michael Bloomberg, cigarette butts account for 75 percent of the litter found on the city's 14 miles (22.5km) of beaches.

- According to Americans for Nonsmokers' Rights, by 2011, 507 American cities and towns had banned smoking in public parks and 105 on public beaches.

CHAPTER ONE

What Are the Origins of the Smoking Ban Controversy?

Television history was made on New Year's night in 1971, when the last commercial for a cigarette brand aired on TV. In the final seconds of the spot, a leggy model peered at the camera, raising a hand to her chin so the viewing public could see a Virginia Slims cigarette held between two fingers.

Four years earlier Congress had passed a measure requiring TV stations to air at least one antismoking public service announcement (PSA) for every three cigarette ads they aired. At the time, tobacco companies were using young and attractive actors and models in their TV ads, filming them in carefree settings at the beach, at parties, aboard pleasure boats, and in all manner of other engaging scenarios, always enjoying cigarettes together. The message to viewers was clear: Smokers were young, beautiful, and hip, and smoking was enjoyed during good times. In fact, the ad slogan for Virginia Slims, which were marketed to women, was "You've come a long way, baby."

In other words, Virginia Slims smokers were independent women who still managed to hold on to their sex appeal. But after the antismoking PSAs started airing, the public saw another side of smoking—sick people suffering from lung cancer or emphysema were often featured. One commercial featured actor William Talman, who played district attorney Hamilton Burger on the crime drama *Perry Mason*, one of the most popular TV shows of the era. During the PSA, which aired in 1968, Talman showed photographs of his wife and 6 children. Talman ended the PSA by disclosing that he suffers from lung cancer and admonishing viewers not to smoke. Talman died 6 weeks after filming the PSA. He was 53 years old.

Total Ban on Advertising

Congress would soon take a far more significant step toward reining in the tobacco industry's use of TV advertising as a medium to sell cigarettes. In 1969 lawmakers in Washington, DC, proposed a total ban on cigarette advertising on TV. The tobacco industry fought hard against the ban but eventually gave in, and on April 1, 1970, President Richard Nixon signed a law prohibiting cigarette advertising on TV. As a concession to the tobacco industry, lawmakers delayed implementation of the ban until January 2, 1971. The delay gave the tobacco companies one last shot at reaching the huge number of TV viewers who watch college football bowl games on New Year's Day.

Moreover, now that there would be no more cigarette ads on TV, it meant the TV networks were under no obligation to run as many of the antismoking PSAs as they had been required to air in the past. To the tobacco companies' way of seeing things, it meant the public would see far fewer lung cancer victims on TV.

And so on that New Year's Day in 1971, the tobacco companies blanketed the airwaves with their commercials, the last airing one minute before midnight. The Virginia Slims commercial aired during *The Tonight Show*, which at the time was hosted by comedian Johnny Carson, one of the most popular entertainers of the era. He enjoyed a huge and dedicated following, much as Jay Leno and David Letterman do today. Each night millions of viewers tuned in, and they invariably saw Carson interviewing celebrity guests while a cigarette burned between his fingers. After 30 years as host of the *Tonight Show*, Carson retired in 1992. Thirteen years later, he died of emphysema.

Automobile mogul Henry Ford (left) whispers in the ear of inventor Thomas Edison. In a 1914 letter, Edison warned Ford about the health dangers of cigarettes.

Harmful to Human Health

In the decades since the ban on TV advertising, Congress as well as state and local governments adopted many laws designed to make it harder for customers to gain access to cigarettes or to find legal places to smoke. Federal, state, and local governments also made tobacco products more expensive by piling huge taxes onto the sales of packs and cartons. This antismoking campaign by lawmakers was sparked by the January 11, 1964, release of the report *Smoking and Health: Report of the Advisory Committee to the Surgeon General of the United States*, which reported that smoking shortens human life, causes lung cancer as well as other types of cancer, and can lead to heart disease and emphysema—all potentially fatal conditions.

Prior to the issuance of the report, there had been suspicions that cigarettes were harmful to human health. As far back as 1914, inventor Thomas Edison was convinced that smoking was unwise. In a letter to his friend, automobile mogul Henry Ford, Edison wrote, "[Cigarette smoke] has a violent action in the nerve centers, producing degeneration of the cells of the brain, which is quite rapid among boys. Unlike most narcotics, this degeneration is permanent and uncontrollable. I employ no person who smokes cigarettes."[9] Edison was an inventor and engineer—human physiology was not his field. Nevertheless, he had correctly identified one of the hazards of smoking: In 1992 French researchers proved that cigarette smoke kills neurons—the cells found in the brain—and helps prevent the formation of new neurons.

> "These two Christians [de Jerez and de Torres] . . . chew or suck and take in with their breath that smoke which dulls the flesh and as it were intoxicates and so they say that they do not feel weariness."[11]
>
> — Christopher Columbus, fifteenth-century New World explorer.

By the time Edison pronounced smoking an unwise and dangerous habit, the tobacco industry had established a firm footing in American culture. Indeed, the story of Christopher Columbus's arrival in the West Indies is taught in every elementary school in the United States. But what is less known about Columbus's arrival in the New World is that on October 12, 1492—the day he set foot on the island of Guanahaní in the Bahamas (which he renamed San Salvador)—the native Indians gave the explorer a gift of fruit and tobacco. Columbus kept the fruit but, unsure of what to do with the dried tobacco leaves, had them heaved overboard.

The First Chain-Smokers

Columbus soon weighed anchor and continued his voyage, arriving 17 days later in Cuba. Upon going ashore, he met more natives and noticed immediately that many held between their fingers, as he wrote in his journal, a "little lighted brand made from a kind of plant whose aroma it was their custom to inhale."[10] Two of his crew members, Rodrigo de Jerez and Luis de Torres, tried the custom themselves, thus becoming the first Europeans to pick up the smoking habit.

In fact, during the three months Columbus and his crew spent in the New World, de Jerez and de Torres not only became the first

Europeans to smoke, they also became the first European chain-smokers. Columbus did not think much of the habit, writing in his log, "These two Christians [de Jerez and de Torres] . . . chew or suck and take in with their breath that smoke which dulls the flesh and as it were intoxicates and so they say that they do not feel weariness."[11]

By observing that his two shipmates were able to ward off weariness by smoking, Columbus was the first European to make note of the energy-enhancing effects of nicotine, a chemical found in tobacco smoke. The explorer also made note of how tobacco dulled the flesh of the two sailors: One well-known side effect of tobacco use is that it can cause skin to turn sallow, or yellowish.

The Riches of Tobacco

Other explorers were not as easily repulsed by tobacco as Columbus. They also witnessed Indians rolling the leaves into tight cylinders and setting them on fire to inhale the smoke, and these explorers were eager to introduce the custom to their home countries. Hernán Cortés returned to Spain in 1518 with a cargo of tobacco. Smoking was introduced to the French in 1556 by a monk, André Thévet, who picked up the habit while on an expedition to Brazil, where the Indians called tobacco leaves *petun*. Said Thévet, "There is a . . . secret herb which they name in their language petun, [and] which they most commonly bear about them for that they esteem it marvelously profitable for many things."[12] From the 1560s through the 1580s, several English explorers, including Sir Francis Drake and Sir Walter Raleigh, brought cargoes of tobacco home to England. These explorers created a tobacco habit among Europeans. To feed that habit, Europeans looked to America.

"There is a . . . secret herb which [Brazilians] name in their language petun, [and] which they most commonly bear about them for that they esteem it marvelously profitable for many things."[12]

— André Thévet, the sixteenth-century monk who introduced smoking in France.

Soon after the Jamestown colony was established in Virginia in 1607, its most successful crop was tobacco. By 1630 Jamestown farmers were exporting 300,000 pounds (136,078kg) of tobacco a year to England. A decade later, annual shipments of tobacco reached 1 million pounds (453,592kg), and by the end of the seventeenth century, tobacco exports from Virginia totaled more than 30 million pounds (13.6 million kg). Said Jamestown colonist John Pory, "All our riches for the present do consist in tobacco."[13]

Tobacco spread across the South, where the warm but rainy climate suited tobacco farmers perfectly. By the start of the Civil War, tobacco was the second-most cultivated crop in the South, following cotton.

Tobacco Goes to War

Even though tobacco was an important American crop, by 1900 relatively few Americans smoked cigarettes. Cigars and pipe tobacco were much more popular. Indeed, by 1900 cigar smoking was so common that consumers could choose from more than 300,000 brands on the market. Meanwhile, a familiar sight in virtually every saloon in America was the spittoon—the ceramic or metal receptacle where patrons could spit out their chewing tobacco. Spittoons could also be found in offices, barber shops, courtrooms, and even some homes. Eventually, the health hazards of cigars, pipe tobacco, and chewing tobacco would also be exposed.

> "All our riches for the present do consist in tobacco."[13]
>
> — Jamestown colonist John Pory.

As for cigarettes, by 1900 American tobacco companies were selling about 4 billion a year—a number that may seem significant, but by the time of the surgeon general's report 64 years later, that number had increased to about 450 billion. Tobacco companies owed much of their success in the early years of the twentieth century to an unlikely benefactor: the American Red Cross. When America entered World War I in 1917, the Red Cross provided care packages to American soldiers—shipping millions of parcels overseas that included chocolate, coffee, and other foods, as well as packages of soap and cigarettes.

As a result, the Red Cross was largely responsible for introducing the addictive powers of nicotine to hundreds of thousands of American men—with the blessing of America's top military commander. "You ask what we need to win this war," declared General John Pershing, who commanded American troops in

Europe. "I answer, tobacco, as much as bullets. Tobacco is as indispensable as the daily ration. We must have thousands of tons of it without delay."[14]

Lack of Medical Research

When American soldiers returned home from Europe, many had developed a cigarette habit. By 1929 tobacco companies were selling 80 billion cigarettes a year to American smokers. Many of these new smokers were women who enjoyed the early fruits of women's liberation in the 1920s: breaking away from the authoritative control of their families to date whomever they pleased, using birth control, drinking alcoholic beverages, and smoking cigarettes.

In the early 1900s, however, a woman who smoked in public could be arrested. Not until 1929 would women be permitted to smoke in railroad dining cars. As the suffragist movement gained traction in the early years of the century, many women marched for their rights. During the marches, it was common for the suffragists to light cigarettes showing that they, too, should have the right to smoke as they pleased. Seizing the opportunity at hand, the manufacturer of Lucky Strike cigarettes dispatched photographers to the suffragist parades to photograph young and attractive models who fell into step with the suffragists, holding up their Lucky Strike cigarettes to show the brand smoked by the truly liberated woman. The photographs were used in Lucky Strike's advertising campaigns.

> "You ask what we need to win this war. I answer, tobacco, as much as bullets. Tobacco is as indispensable as the daily ration. We must have thousands of tons of it without delay."[14]
>
> — General John Pershing, who commanded US troops during World War I.

The 1920s was the era of Prohibition, when the sale and consumption of alcoholic beverages were illegal under the law. Many states legislatures recognized cigarette smoking as hazardous and attempted to enact prohibitions on cigarettes as well. These laws met with as much success as the alcohol ban: They were, for the most part, widely ignored, and cigarette sales continued to increase. A reason for the failure of these laws was the lack of medical data supporting the belief that smoking could be dangerous. For example, a University of Minnesota study of the era found that of 3,399 deaths that occurred between 1899 and 1919, just four could be attributed to lung cancer. Not until the 1950s would medical researchers start building the case that cigarette smoking is hazardous to human health.

The Surgeon General's Report

Scientific research proving the dangers of smoking was finally published in the 1964 report by Surgeon General Luther Terry. The report found that men who smoke cigarettes risk a death rate from disease that is 1,000 times the rate of men who do not smoke, and it specifically cited lung cancer as the primary disease associated with cigarette smoking. In addition, the surgeon general's report said smoking heightens the likelihood of contracting emphysema, a bloating of the lungs that makes breathing difficult and is potentially fatal. The report also stated that smoking could lead to bronchitis, an inflammation of the air passages in the lungs. Terry's report also said people who smoke harbor a risk of suffering heart disease that is 70 percent higher than nonsmokers. Cancers found in the bladder as well as the esophagus, the channel connecting the mouth to the stomach, were also linked to smoking.

The report said cigarette smoke contains a high concentration of polycyclic aromatic hydrocarbons, chemicals containing carbon and hydrogen that are carcinogenic (meaning they can cause cancer). These chemicals were grouped together into a category of substances known as "tar." The report also cited the presence of nicotine, the chemical that causes cigarettes to be habit-forming and creates the body's craving for smoking. Said the report, "Cigarette smoking is a health hazard of sufficient importance in the United States to warrant appropriate remedial action."[15]

The report also looked at pipe smoking and cigar use, finding the health effects to be less pronounced—but some concerns were raised. Pipe smoking, for example, was cited as a cause of lip cancer. The report also found that death rates for people who smoke five or more cigars a day were higher than for nonsmokers. Terry's report did not address smokeless tobacco, but a 1986 report by Surgeon General C. Everett Koop said using smokeless tobacco could cause cancerous tumors to form in the mouth and throat as well as the esophagus.

The 1964 surgeon general's report contained the first warning about smoking during pregnancy, finding that pregnant women who smoke tend to give birth to smaller babies. The report devoted little space to the issue. However, later that year physician and anthropologist Ashley Montagu published a landmark book on prenatal care titled *Life Before Birth*. In that book he declared that smoking leads to lower birth weight as well as premature deliveries,

The Triangle Shirtwaist Factory Fire

One of the first laws to restrict smoking indoors was adopted well before the health hazards of smoking were known. Rather, New York State's Sullivan-Hoey Fire Prevention Law of 1911 was adopted following the tragic fire at the Triangle Shirtwaist Factory in New York City, which claimed the lives of 146 workers, mostly women who worked in the building. (A shirtwaist is a woman's blouse.)

Smoking had been prohibited in the building by the factory's owners, but the rule was generally ignored. On March 25, 1911, it is believed a worker carelessly tossed a lit cigarette or cigar onto the factory floor, sparking the blaze. The fire quickly engulfed the locked building, trapping the workers inside. The New York State Legislature acted quickly following the blaze, passing the Sullivan-Hoey measure that established the New York Bureau of Fire Protection. The bureau was given wide powers to ensure similar tragedies did not occur, and as a result of these new powers the owners of businesses judged to be fire hazards were required to follow this rule: "You are . . . ordered to prohibit and prevent the smoking of any pipe, cigar or cigarette in the work rooms, stock rooms, packing rooms, toilet rooms, passageways or any other part of the above described premises at any time or by any person."

Quoted in Peter Joseph McKeon, *Fire Prevention: A Treatise and Textbook on Making Life and Property Safe Against Fire*. New York: Chief, 1912, p. 218.

both factors that could lead to children born with physical and mental handicaps. "[There is] no question at all that smoking is harmful to a child before birth, and the implication is clear for a pregnant woman who is also a smoker: stop smoking," wrote Montagu. "A prospective mother who is genuinely interested in the welfare of her child does not wait for 'proof'; the bare possibility that she may be hurting her child is enough to give her a reason to stop smoking."[16]

Warnings on Labels

The first legislation adopted in response to the surgeon general's report was signed into law by President Lyndon Johnson on January 1, 1966. It required tobacco companies to print a warning on cigarette packages stating, "Caution: Cigarette Smoking May Be Hazardous to Your Health."[17] However, the warning as well as the widespread publicity reporting the dangers of smoking had just a minor impact on American tobacco use. In 1966, the last year before the warnings appeared on cigarette packs and cartons, the average American smoker consumed 11.8 cigarettes a day. By the end of 1967, a year after the warnings appeared, cigarette usage by smokers had barely dropped—smokers were still burning through 11.7 cigarettes a day.

> "A prospective mother who is genuinely interested in the welfare of her child does not wait for 'proof'; the bare possibility that she may be hurting her child is enough to give her a reason to stop smoking."[16]
>
> — Physician and anthropologist Ashley Montagu.

Clearly, the warning labels were not doing their job, which is why Congress passed the ban on TV advertising. In 1970, the last full year of cigarette commercials on TV, tobacco companies spent more than $200 million to advertise their products on the American airwaves. (In today's dollars, that equates to about $1.1 billion.) Tobacco companies responded to the ban by moving their advertising dollars to other media—newspapers, magazines, billboards, and similar forms of promotion. They hired the nation's top advertising agencies to plan these ad campaigns, which basically mirrored the TV campaigns that had long been familiar to Americans. Smokers were still portrayed as young, physically attractive, fun loving, and hip.

High Taxes and the Tobacco Habit

In 2009 Congress mandated a tax hike on cigarettes, raising the federal levy from 39 cents per pack to $1.01 per pack. According to Matthew McKenna, director of the Office on Smoking and Health for the CDC, the federal hike raised the average price of a pack of cigarettes in most states by about 10 percent. (States assess their own taxes, which is why the cost of a pack of cigarettes varies greatly from state to state, ranging from less than $5 in West Virginia to nearly $12 in New York State.)

According to McKenna, statistics show that when the price of a pack of cigarettes is raised by 10 percent, about a million people respond by giving up the habit. The 2009 tax hike came close to achieving that number. The CDC reported that in 2008—the year before the tax hike went into effect—46 million Americans smoked cigarettes. In 2010, after the new tax had been in effect for a year, the CDC's statistics showed that 700,000 fewer Americans continued to smoke cigarettes.

By the 1980s it seemed as though the TV advertising ban had little effect on the American smoking habit. By 1980 American tobacco companies were churning out some 650 billion cigarettes a year—about 100 billion more per year than they produced in 1970, the final year before the TV ban. Consequently, in 1985 Congress mandated that cigarette packages and cartons carry new warning labels containing much harsher messages. Moreover, these messages were also mandated to appear conspicuously in print advertising for cigarette brands. Among the messages are "Smoking Causes Lung Cancer, Heart Disease, Emphysema, and May Complicate Pregnancy" as well as "Quitting Smoking Now Greatly Reduces Serious Risks to Your Health." Another warning label reads, "Smoking by Pregnant Women May Result in Fetal Injury."[18]

A factory worker sorts cigarette packs at R.J. Reynolds Tobacco Company in the 1970s. By 1980, US tobacco companies were producing 650 billion cigarettes a year.

The legislation mandating the new and tougher warning labels on cigarette packs and cartons was signed into law by President Ronald Reagan. (Before entering politics, Reagan pursued a career as a film star. Although he was a nonsmoker, during his acting career Reagan appeared in many advertisements for Chesterfield cigarettes.)

The Tobacco Suit

By 1990 sales of cigarettes had finally started slipping. That year Americans burned through about 550 billion a year—100 billion less than the peak year of 1980. The reduction was likely due in part to the combined efforts of the federal and state governments to curtail cigarette use through mandates requiring warning labels, advertising restrictions, and the imposition of heavy taxes. However, the states had no power to ban advertising or mandate that cigarette packs carry warning labels, but they could levy taxes on cigarettes, making them much more expensive to the consumer.

Although states had been taxing cigarette sales since the 1920s—Iowa was the first to enact a tax on cigarette sales in 1921—by the mid-1960s cigarettes were still inexpensive. In most states a pack of cigarettes would cost the consumer about 40 cents. But cigarette taxes started rising by leaps and bounds in the 1970s. Moreover, the federal government added its own taxes, and some cities levied taxes on cigarette sales as well. Today the average cost of a pack of cigarettes varies from state to state, ranging from $4.74 in West Virginia to $11.90 in New York.

Starting in the 1970s, states and communities passed other measures as well, most notably the laws banning cigarette smoking in government buildings. In 2002 Delaware became the first state to enact a complete ban on smoking in restaurants and taverns; since then, most other states have enacted similar measures. Employers adopted their own rules, banning cigarette smoking inside offices, factories, and other places of employment. Meanwhile, the states developed a new strategy. In 1994 the state attorneys general started suing the tobacco companies. They claimed diseases caused by cigarette smoking greatly inflated the burden on taxpayers to fund Medicaid—the joint state and federal program that funds health care for poor people. Eventually, 46 states joined what became a common lawsuit against the tobacco industry. The nation's four largest tobacco companies—Philip Morris USA, R.J. Reynolds Tobacco Company, Brown & Williamson Tobacco Corporation, and Lorillard Tobacco Company—fought the case for four years. In 1998 they agreed to settle with the states, providing a $246 billion fund the states could tap for antismoking campaigns and to help fund their Medicaid costs. The fund is payable over a period of 25 years.

If tobacco industry executives believed the settlement from

the 1994 lawsuit would end the government siege on cigarettes, they were wrong. In the first two decades of the twenty-first century, local and state governments as well as the federal government have continued to adopt laws and regulations aimed at limiting smoking. In 2009 a new federal tax on cigarettes went into effect, raising the federal levy on a pack from 39 cents to $1.01.

Meanwhile, laws intended to limit cigarette advertising in the nonelectronic media have been enacted. In 2001 Massachusetts lawmakers banned cigarette advertising on billboards and other outside venues near schools. The tobacco companies challenged the law and this time won—the US Supreme Court ruled the law was too vague. A decade later, though, the town of Worcester, Massachusetts, adopted a local ordinance banning stores from displaying cigarette advertisements in their windows. "About five people a week die in Worcester from tobacco, compared to a total of 42 people in all of 2009 who died in car crashes in all of Worcester County," says Worcester city solicitor David Moore. "If we were talking about five people dying a week from pharmaceuticals, no one would say government doesn't have some kind of role in trying to regulate [drugs]."[19]

Common Siege on Smoking

During the twentieth century, the US government dramatically changed its position on smoking from bullish support to outright hostility. Soon after the century started, Pershing declared that cigarettes were vital to the war effort in Europe, and the American Red Cross responded by shipping millions overseas. But by the end of the century, the federal government as well as state and city governments began to join what has become a common siege on tobacco use. Clearly, their efforts were prompted by the surgeon general's report of 1964 that declared cigarette smoking and other forms of tobacco use to be a health hazard. Nevertheless, in 2011 a *Wall Street Journal* report noted that Americans still smoke 300 billion cigarettes a year—a statistic that might suggest to lawmakers they still have plenty of work left to do.

Facts

- Since the release of the original 1964 report *Smoking and Health: Report of the Advisory Committee to the Surgeon General of the United States*, various US surgeons general have subsequently issued another 29 reports on tobacco use, all presenting new scientific evidence on the dangers of smoking.

- The 2010 version of the surgeon general's report on smoking, titled *A Report of the Surgeon General: How Tobacco Smoke Causes Disease*, identified 7,000 chemicals in tobacco smoke, 69 of which are carcinogenic.

- According to a 2012 report by the American Lung Association, New York State assesses the highest tax on cigarettes at $4.25 per pack, whereas Missouri's levy of 17 cents per pack is the lowest state tax assessed on cigarettes.

- Only two states raised their cigarette taxes in 2011, according to the American Lung Association. Those states were Vermont, which hiked its tax by 38 cents per pack, and Connecticut, which raised its tax by 40 cents.

- According to the antismoking group Campaign for Tobacco-Free Kids, by 2011 just $7.2 billion of the $246 billion 1998 tobacco settlement had been paid to state governments. A 2008 report on National Public Radio said a lot of states have devoted the money to fixing roads, building schools, and balancing budgets, rather than devoting the funds to antismoking programs.

CHAPTER TWO

Have Bans on Youth Cigarette Sales Affected Teen Smoking Rates?

Laura, a 17-year-old high school student from Vernon Hills, Illinois, started smoking at the age of 13. All her friends smoked; to fit in, she tried cigarettes as well. "I started smoking because I thought everyone was doing it, and I wanted to be able to do it too," Laura told the magazine *Current Health 2*. "Then, it was something to do; I guess I was bored. At first, I liked it. It seemed to calm me down, but then I got addicted. I should have quit before then."[20]

"I started smoking because I thought everyone was doing it, and I wanted to be able to do it too."[20]

— Laura, a 17-year-old Illinois high school student.

Eventually, Laura was smoking a pack of cigarettes a day—with predictably unpleasant results. She soon developed a "smoker's cough" as well as wheezing in her lungs—both common side effects of tobacco use. She also did not like the odor of cigarette smoke in her hair, in her clothes, and on her breath. Laura worries about the long-term health risks, so she has resolved to quit. She has cut down to about a half dozen cigarettes a day and hopes to totally quit the habit by the time she reaches the age of 18. In her quest to quit smoking, her boyfriend—an ex-smoker—is giving her plenty of moral support. "He doesn't pressure me to quit but supports me," Laura says. "He'd like me to live a long time. Sometimes, when I smoke around him, I feel like an idiot."[21]

Get-Tough Policies

It is ironic that Laura has resolved to quit smoking by her eighteenth birthday, because that is the age at which she would be legally permitted to smoke. Every one of those cigarettes she has smoked from the age of 13 was obtained illegally, because Illinois banned the sale of cigarettes to minors in 1983. Illinois is not alone; all 50 states prohibit the sale of cigarettes to people under the age of 18. Four states—Alabama, Alaska, New Jersey, and Utah—have banned sales of cigarettes to people under the age of 19. Moreover, three counties in New York State—Onondaga, Nassau, and Suffolk—have passed local ordinances mandating bans on cigarette sales to customers under the age of 19. Retailers who sell cigarettes to minors face fines or jail sentences, depending on the provisions of their states' laws.

In addition, 46 states have made it a crime for minors to possess cigarettes. Young people arrested for cigarette possession in those states could face fines. Only New York State, Massachusetts, Nevada, and New Jersey have not passed youth possession laws.

States began establishing laws regulating the sales of cigarettes to minors in the early 1900s, but they were rarely enforced—at least not with much vigor. For decades a common sight on city streets was a gang of young toughs loitering on the sidewalk, cigarettes dangling from their mouths. Following the surgeon general's 1964 report, states started cracking down, passing stricter laws and putting their resources behind enforcement. Over the years, the percentage of young people who smoke has decreased—but it has taken decades to show results. According to Monitoring the Future, a University of Michigan project that charts substance abuse by young people, in 1975 a stunning 73 percent of high school seniors were believed to have smoked cigarettes in their lifetimes. By 2011 that number had dropped to 40 percent.

All 50 states prohibit the sale of cigarettes to people under the age of 18, with some states and counties setting the threshold for legal purchase at 19. To help monitor sales, many stores place cigarettes in locked cabinets.

Of course, high school seniors are not the only young people who smoke—as Laura's case illustrates, many young people typically start smoking as they reach early adolescence. Nationally, according to the CDC, almost 17.2 percent of all high school students have at least experimented with cigarettes—meaning that nearly 1 in 5 people under the age of 18 have inhaled tobacco smoke. Therefore, even though the states have adopted get-tough policies against underage smoking, plenty of retailers are still ignoring the laws in favor of making profits from the sales of cigarettes to underage smokers.

Sting Operations

Most states require retailers to demand identification from cigarette buyers if they appear to be underage—much as liquor retailers are required to ask for identification from buyers they suspect to be under the age of 21, the national minimum legal drinking age. To enforce the laws against sales of cigarettes to minors, authorities often conduct random inspections of stores, in which undercover investigators observe the cashiers to determine whether they are selling cigarettes to minors. It is not unusual for investigators to run sting operations—drafting local young people and sending them into stores to buy cigarettes.

That is what happened in Santa Barbara County, California, in 2011, when the county's Department of Health, with the assistance of local police, sent underage "decoys" into 275 stores. During the sting operation, the underage buyers were able to purchase cigarettes in nearly 50 stores—about a 17 percent rate. The highest rate in the county was recorded in the town of Lompoc, where cashiers in 9 of 29 stores—a 31 percent rate—sold cigarettes to minors. "That's very discouraging," says Lompoc police chief Tim Dabney, who promised to continue the tobacco stings. "I would like to see it back down to zero."[22]

Nationally, the crackdowns have shown some results. According to the Substance Abuse and Mental Health Services Administration (SAMHSA), the percentage of retailers cited for selling tobacco to minors fell to an all-time low in 2010, when 9.3 percent of retailers that were inspected were charged with breaking the law. In 2009, 10.9 percent of inspected retailers were found to be selling cigarettes to minors—an increase over the previous year's statistic of 9.9 percent.

The Family Smoking Prevention and Tobacco Control Act

SAMHSA officials attributed the 2010 drop to the 2009 Family Smoking Prevention and Tobacco Control Act, which provided the US Food and Drug Administration (FDA) with funding to help states conduct compliance checks. As a result, more compliance checks are conducted today than in the past because there is now more money available to run the stings. The 2009 law gave widespread authority to the FDA to curb smoking by young people. "This is a bill not for a one-year or two-year splash, but for

Does Smoking Deserve an R Rating?

Movie fans under the age of 17 may one day need to be accompanied to theaters by an adult if they expect to see films in which the characters are depicted smoking cigarettes. According to a 2007 study cosponsored by the antismoking advocacy group American Legacy Foundation and the Dartmouth-Hitchcock Medical Center in New Hampshire, young people who are exposed to depictions of smoking in movies double their risk of picking up the habit themselves.

The Motion Picture Association of America (MPAA) responded to the study by assigning a PG-13 rating to movies in which characters are depicted smoking. The rating alerts parents that some material in the film may be inappropriate for viewers under the age of 13.

The American Legacy Foundation does not believe the MPAA's action went far enough and has demanded that films depicting tobacco use be assigned an R rating, meaning viewers under the age of 17 must be accompanied by an adult to gain admittance to the theater. "What we need to do to affect meaningful change is to keep smoking out of the G, PG and PG-13 films currently influencing our youth," says Cheryl Heaton, president of the American Legacy Foundation.

Quoted in Brooks Boliek, "Study Hits Screen Smoke," *Hollywood Reporter*, September 6, 2007, p. 6.

a long-term impact,"[23] says Matthew L. Myers, president of the Campaign for Tobacco-Free Kids.

The law is intended to limit the access of young people to tobacco products by providing the states with funds to run sting operations and other enforcement methods to ensure cigarettes are not sold to underage smokers. Another provision of the law bans cigarette vending machines in places where people under the age of 18 are permitted to enter, such as diners, bowling alleys, and amusement parks. The law went even further, not only limiting access by young people to tobacco products, but also to the types of products that tend to be popular among teens—such as T-shirts, baseball caps, and other items that are emblazoned with tobacco company logos and similar promotional images. Finally, the law prohibits tobacco company sponsorship of rock concerts and similar events that young fans are likely to attend.

Essentially, the law provides yet another crackdown on cigarette advertising, only in this case the ads appeared not on TV but on T-shirts, baseball caps, or video screens at rock concerts. Myers says he is sure the law will prove to be an effective tool in reducing tobacco use by young people. He points out that a 2010 study by the antismoking group American Legacy Foundation found that the R.J. Reynolds brand Camel No. 9 is particularly popular among teenage girls. The study reported that Reynolds advertises the brand primarily in *Vogue*, *Cosmopolitan*, and *Glamour*—magazines that are often read by teenage girls. The cigarettes are packaged and marketed in a pink color scheme, which the study found is appealing to girls. The American Legacy Foundation interviewed 1,036 girls between the ages of 12 and 16 and found many of them able to identify the brand, with 22 percent stating the Camel No. 9 ad is their favorite cigarette ad. According to John Pierce, associate director of the Moores Cancer Center at the University of California–San Diego, when teenagers can identify a cigarette brand through its advertising, they are 50 percent more likely to start smoking than other young people.

> *"The continuing high rates of youth tobacco use and the vast sums spent on tobacco marketing are directly related."*[24]
>
> — Matthew L. Myers, president of the Campaign for Tobacco-Free Kids.

Myers insists the Camel No. 9 campaign is directed toward young smokers and that the FDA would do well to use the law to end tobacco advertising campaigns that it finds are aimed at making teenagers into smokers. "The continuing high rates of youth tobacco use and the vast sums spent on tobacco marketing are directly related," Myers says. "The need for these marketing restrictions is clear."[24]

Tobacco Advertising Bans Ineffective

David Howard, a spokesperson for R.J. Reynolds, defends the advertising campaign, arguing that 85 percent of the readers of *Vogue*, *Cosmopolitan*, and *Glamour* are over the age of 18. Other critics of the law defend the tobacco companies as well, arguing that over the years, the various bans on cigarette advertising seem to have had little impact on young smokers. Patrick Basham, director of the Democracy Institute, a Washington, DC–based organization that advocates for fewer governmental regulations, points out that CDC statistics show that a significant number of young people have picked up the cigarette habit. This has occurred despite their growing into adolescence in an era in which cigarette advertising on TV has been banned and harshly worded warning labels appear on cigarette packages and print ads.

"The evidence in support of tobacco display bans, just as for tobacco advertising bans, is embarrassingly thin. Most studies show that tobacco displays have no statistically significant effect on youth smoking."[25]

— Patrick Basham, director of the Democracy Institute.

According to CDC statistics, in 2006, 19.8 percent of high school students had at least experimented with tobacco, with many becoming regular smokers. That number may have dropped to 17.2 percent in 2009, but Basham categorizes that drop as a minor and statistically insignificant decrease that does not prove the effectiveness of advertising bans on young people. "The evidence in support of tobacco display bans, just as for tobacco advertising bans, is embarrassingly thin," he says. "Most studies show that tobacco displays have no statistically significant effect on youth smoking."[25]

The Era of Joe Camel

The notion that tobacco companies regard young people as consumers is not a new idea. Even before the issuance of the 1964 surgeon general's report, children were exposed to messages from the tobacco companies that seemed especially tailored for their interests. In 1960, for example, the ABC television network premiered the animated children's show *The Flintstones*. The show was sponsored by Winston cigarettes and featured commercials in which the character Fred Flintstone lit a Winston for his wife, Wilma, and enjoyed smoking with his friend Barney Rubble.

By the 1990s the tobacco companies found themselves under pressure from antismoking advocates, federal officials, and the

Banning Tobacco Lozenges

In 2011 tobacco companies test-marketed tobacco lozenges, which are candies that contain tobacco as a key ingredient. Among these products are Camel Orbs by R.J. Reynolds as well as Ariva and Stonewall by Star Scientific. A year after these products were test-marketed, the FDA said it would consider a ban on them.

Jonathan Winickoff, a pediatrician at Massachusetts General Hospital in Boston, says tobacco lozenges have appeal to young people. "If you wanted to design a product that would appeal to youth and addict younger adolescents . . . to nicotine, this would be it," says Winickoff. "These products are designed to look like a candy and addict the user permanently."

Winickoff says the lozenges give people the same rush from nicotine that cigarettes provide. Moreover, he says, teens would find they can pop the lozenges in their mouths and not worry about the odor of smoke on their breath or their clothes. "Just because they smell like chocolate or mint and look safe, they contain nicotine and are potentially harmful for adolescents and could start a lifetime of nicotine addiction," he says.

Winickoff says swallowing a lozenge whole could lead to nicotine poisoning. Symptoms of nicotine poisoning include vomiting, nausea, diarrhea, and headache. Severe nicotine poisoning can include muscle paralysis and seizures, which could be fatal.

Quoted in Denise Mann, "FDA to Weigh Safety of Tobacco Lozenges, Strips," *USA Today*, January 18, 2012. http://yourlife.usatoday.com.

states' lawsuit to admit that they had spent years targeting young people as potential smokers. No episode better exemplified that strategy than the Joe Camel advertising campaign launched in 1987 by R.J. Reynolds for its Camel brand of cigarettes.

The campaign featured a young and hip character who lounged at the beach, played billiards, and rode motorcycles. His image was often portrayed under the headline "Smooth Character"—a message intended to convey the taste of the cigarette as well as the attitude of the smoker. In all the company's advertisements, the character was portrayed with a Camel cigarette dangling from his lips.

> "Joe Camel was just the sort of slightly older figure whom young boys idolize: he was aggressively independent, fun-loving, and eager to flout authority."[26]
>
> — Allan M. Brandt, professor of medical history at Harvard University.

The main difference between this character and the other smokers portrayed in cigarette ads was that the new marketing icon for Camel cigarettes was a cartoon caricature of a camel. He was named Joe Camel, and he was intended to update what had become an old and staid brand—Camel cigarettes were first introduced into the American market in 1913. A 1986 market study indicated to the company that Camel smokers were mostly in their sixties; at the time, most younger smokers preferred Marlboro cigarettes, a competing brand manufactured by Philip Morris. The advertising icon for Marlboro was the Marlboro Man, a rugged and taciturn cowboy who rode tall in the saddle and smoked Marlboro cigarettes. (David McLean, Wayne McClaren, and Dick Hammer, the three actors who portrayed the Marlboro man in the company's commercials, all died of lung cancer.)

Given the popularity of Marlboro cigarettes, from R.J. Reynolds's point of view the Camel brand needed to be updated and aimed at a wider—and younger—market. Moreover, the company needed a symbol for its brand that it hoped could rise to a level of popularity that would match the Marlboro Man. The solution was Joe Camel. Allan M. Brandt, a professor of medical history at Harvard University, says:

> Soon, [Joe Camel's] face was everywhere: in newspapers and magazines, on billboards and posters, and on all man-

ner of apparel and products in the form of decals and logos. Joe Camel was just the sort of slightly older figure whom young boys idolize: he was aggressively independent, fun-loving, and eager to flout authority. . . . Whether wearing shades and playing pool at a nightclub or out for the night in formal wear, he was the ultimate party animal. . . . He was never seen without a cigarette dangling from his elongated snout.[26]

Targeting Children

Antismoking activists soon took notice of Joe Camel and charged that Reynolds's real intention was to entice adolescents to start smoking. Critics of the campaign included President Bill Clinton, who declared, "We must put tobacco ads like Joe Camel out of our children's reach forever."[27]

In fact, there was significant evidence that adolescents were drawn to Camel cigarettes. A 1991 study by the American Medical

Joe Camel, pictured in a flashy wall mural in the 1990s, conveyed an image of independence, fun, and coolness that appealed to young adult males—exactly the group R.J. Reynolds needed to attract to keep its products selling.

Association found that following the inception of the Joe Camel advertising campaign, the under-18 market for Camel cigarettes—in other words, the number of young people who were breaking the law to smoke the brand—rose from less than 1 percent of that age group to nearly 33 percent. "They were targeting children," declares US Representative Henry Waxman of California. "At the level of the chief executive officer and the board, they were implementing this strategy."[28]

Bowing to heavy pressure, Reynolds withdrew the Joe Camel campaign in 1997. A year later, when the tobacco companies reached their landmark $246 billion settlement with the states, the state attorneys general wanted to ensure that characters like Joe Camel would never surface again. As part of the settlement, the tobacco companies agreed not to use cartoon figures in their future advertising campaigns.

Banning Flavored Cigarettes

By acting under the authority of the Family Smoking Prevention and Tobacco Control Act, the FDA has taken other steps besides prohibiting tobacco companies from sponsoring rock concerts and giving out free baseball caps featuring their logos. In 2009 the FDA banned flavored cigarettes, some of which included candy-like flavors or the flavor of cloves, which critics had long charged were aimed at enticing youths to smoke. For years tobacco companies had flavored some of their brands, giving them such names as Winter Mocha Mint and Warm Winter Toffee. Lawrence Dayton, head of the FDA's Center for Tobacco Products, says that flavored cigarettes are often favored by teen smokers. "Studies show that 17-year-old smokers are three times as likely to use flavored cigarettes as smokers over the age of 25,"[29] he says.

R.J. Reynolds spokesperson Fred McConnell insists that flavored cigarettes were not aimed at young smokers. "We adhere to strict marketing practices," he says. "We don't market to youth. We don't market

"We don't market to youth. We don't market to adults who don't smoke. We don't encourage people who smoke and quit to smoke again."[30]

— R.J. Reynolds Tobacco spokesperson Fred McConnell.

to adults who don't smoke. We don't encourage people who smoke and quit to smoke again."[30] Nevertheless, the ban was implemented, removing flavored cigarettes from the American market.

America's Smoking Culture

Even as the FDA cracks down on tobacco marketing aimed at young smokers as well as on the manufacture of flavored cigarettes, young people continue to smoke. Despite constant messages about the health hazards of smoking preached to young people by physicians, educators, and public service groups, many teenagers still think it is cool to smoke. Given that there is still something of a smoking culture in America, in which popular characters on TV and in the movies are seen smoking cigarettes, many experts believe that young people today do what young people have been doing for generations—emulate the habits of their role models.

For several years one of the most popular programs on TV has been *Mad Men*, a drama about the hectic and high-pressure world of New York advertising executives in the 1960s. Critics have applauded the show for its accurate depiction of the world of high-stakes advertising in the 1960s—including the fact that the main characters are portrayed as chain-smokers, which was typical for the era. One antismoking advocate who has noticed the appeal of *Mad Men* on young viewers is Kathryn Joosten, a star of the TV drama *Desperate Housewives*. A former smoker, Joosten was diagnosed with lung cancer in 2001; she underwent seven years of treatment before she was declared cancer free. "They should at least have a disclaimer in the front of the show saying smoking is relevant to the time and place and it's not recommended because it causes cancer,"[31] she says.

In fact, the tobacco industry has long benefited from the hip and sexy allure smoking holds over young people. Antismoking activists cringe every time photos appear in the news or on the Internet of popular stars enjoying cigarettes. After watching model Kate Moss smoke while strutting down the catwalk at a fashion show, British newspaper columnist Janice Turner commented, "You have to be intensely beautiful these days to make smoking glamorous."[32]

Raising the Legal Smoking Age to 21

Given the allure that smoking still holds for many young people, many lawmakers feel their job is not finished. With nearly one in five teenagers still smoking cigarettes, several states have considered following the lead of Alabama, Alaska, New Jersey, and Utah and raising their minimum smoking age to 19, and some state lawmakers have introduced bills to raise their minimum smoking age to 21. "These days we're looking at what researchers say works, which is keeping young people from starting cigarette smoking," says Rhoda Perry, a Rhode Island state senator who introduced a bill in her state's legislature to hike the legal smoking age to 21. "Studies have revealed that the longer a young person is kept from smoking, the less likely he or she is to start."[33]

Other activists have called for a federal law that would establish a national smoking age of 21—similar to the National Minimum Drinking Age Act that was established in 1984. Says Laurence Steinberg, a psychologist at Temple University in Philadelphia, "Perhaps anti-smoking education has done about as much as it can be realistically expected to accomplish. We should not discontinue it, of course. But we need some other strategies. At the top of the list should be raising the minimum legal age for purchasing tobacco to 21."[34]

Critics of the movement to raise the legal smoking age suggest that people who are 18 and over are adults in the eyes of the law and are therefore old enough to make their own decisions, including decisions that affect their own health. "Eighteen is the age of majority," says Steven Brown, executive director of the Rhode Island chapter of the American Civil Liberties Union (ACLU). "An 18-year-old is legally an adult and can marry, enter into contracts and serve in the military, so he or she should be able to smoke cigarettes. . . . It is a discrimination against young adults solely on the basis of their age. It's a protective measure that refuses to recognize that 18-year-olds are adults and should generally be treated as such."[35]

As lawmakers in Rhode Island and other states debate the issue of raising their legal smoking age to 21, young people still find ways to obtain cigarettes and pick up the smoking habit. The fact that more than 30 percent of retailers in places like Lompoc, California, are willing to sell cigarettes to minors is a troubling statistic for local officials in Lompoc, as well as for California lawmakers and officials of the FDA, who have been granted new powers to crack down on smoking by young people. In the future, communities like Lompoc are likely to see more sting operations. On the state and federal levels, officials have indicated they will look for new ways to limit tobacco marketing to teenagers as well as take other steps that would make it increasingly difficult for young people to obtain cigarettes.

Facts

- **A 2010 study commissioned by the Philadelphia City Council found that 80 percent of the city's 4,398 stores that sell tobacco are located within 1,000 feet (305m) of a school. Council members reacted to the report by hiking the fine on sales of tobacco to minors from $100 to $250.**
- **According to a 2010 report by Surgeon General Regina Benjamin, each day 4,000 American teenagers—or nearly 1.5 million a year—light up a cigarette for the first time.**
- **The American Lung Association reported in 2012 that the state with the highest rate of teen smokers is Kentucky, where 26.6 percent of high school students smoke cigarettes. The state with the lowest rate is Utah, where 8.5 percent of high school students are smokers.**
- **Monitoring the Future, the University of Michigan project that charts substance abuse by young people, reported in 2011 that 6.1 percent of American eighth-grade students have smoked cigarettes.**
- **The 2011 Monitoring the Future study reported that 51.9 percent of eighth-grade students and 73.6 percent of tenth-grade students find cigarettes either fairly easy or very easy to buy.**

CHAPTER THREE

Do Smoking Bans Violate the Rights of Smokers?

Trapped in a city in which she believes her rights are in a constant state of erosion, Audrey Silk has decided to take a stand. Silk is founder and president of New York City Citizens Lobbying Against Smoker Harassment, or NYC CLASH. The longtime smoker has testified before New York City Council meetings, spoken out in the media, and in 2011 organized a rally along the boardwalk in the city's resort-like Coney Island neighborhood. NYC CLASH staged the rally to protest the city ordinance that prohibits smoking in city-owned parks and beaches. "When the law is an ass, it's our duty to revolt,"[36] Silk declared as the rally got underway.

Activists like Silk insist that smokers also have rights and that governments should not ignore their needs. "They're using the force of law to socially engineer the public," she says. "It should be up to each individual. It's a legal product. For a government to step in and make it as difficult and expensive as it is, they are more than overreaching their role."[37]

In the decades since the 1964 surgeon general's report, the places where smoking is permitted have been greatly reduced, while the taxes charged on packs and cartons of cigarettes have skyrocketed—boosting the cost of cigarettes. And yet, according to the CDC, 20.6 percent of adults—some 45.3 million people—continue to smoke cigarettes.

Several smoking advocacy groups like NYC CLASH have formed, and their leaders insist that people who smoke are still using legal products and should not be harassed by the government. "Tobacco and smoking are legal," insists Silk. "Now leave me alone to make my informed decision as an adult."[38]

Cigarette Breaks

One trend that has smokers concerned is the movement by many employers to end cigarette breaks. When private employers started mandating smoke-free workplaces in the 1980s and 1990s, it meant that workers could no longer smoke at their desks, on factory floors, in teachers' lounges, or anywhere else inside the workplace. As a result, smokers soon started drifting outside for cigarette breaks. Many employers acknowledged the practice and tacitly agreed to permit employees to take brief cigarette breaks. It was not unusual for some employers to designate specific outdoor smoking areas on company property and provide benches and ash receptacles for smokers to use.

In recent years, though, many companies have become far less tolerant of cigarette breaks, finding that some of their employees abuse the privilege. Many employers are also forced to endure the complaints of workers who do not smoke. These workers contend that they deserve equal time away from their jobs. In 2011 the Washington, DC–based advocacy group Action on Smoking and Health reported that the typical smoker takes four 15-minute cigarette breaks during an 8-hour shift. Therefore, the typical smoker is spending an hour's worth of company time each day on a cigarette break—or about 240 hours a year devoted to smoking. This means a smoker who works full-time is spending the equivalent of 30 days a year standing outside with a burning cigarette rather than at his or her work station. Over the course of an employment career that could last 40 years, this could mean that a typical employee who takes smoking breaks will spend the equivalent

> "Tobacco and smoking are legal. Now leave me alone to make my informed decision as an adult."[38]
>
> — Smokers' rights activist Audrey Silk.

of 1,200 days—or more than three years—smoking cigarettes on company time.

Those are the types of statistics that have prompted many employers to ban cigarette breaks. For example, the Rochester, New York, law firm of Dibble & Miller had for years permitted employees to take brief smoking breaks of no more than a few minutes. In 2006, after several employees were found to be abusing the policy—drawing their smoking breaks out to as long as a half hour at a time—the firm declared that cigarette breaks would no longer be allowed. "You try to lay back and be nice to employees," says Gerald Dibble, a partner in the firm. "I don't know how an employer could allow a person who smokes to take breaks and not give that same benefit to another employee."[39]

"I don't know how an employer could allow a person who smokes to take breaks and not give that same benefit to another employee."[39]

— Rochester, New York, attorney Gerald Dibble, who banned cigarette breaks by employees of his law firm.

One employee defied the Dibble & Miller ban. Paralegal Karen Kridel was fired after she continued to take brief smoking breaks in the mornings and afternoons. Kridel appealed her firing to a New York State court, contending that she was spending no more than five minutes at a time during her smoking breaks and was making up for the breaks by working late and returning from lunch early. But the court upheld her firing, finding that she violated her employer's legal right to ban smoking breaks on company time. Perhaps Kridel did not help her case when she argued that people who smoke need to satisfy their nicotine addictions because if they do not, they can become moody and unpleasant around coworkers. "Within an eight-hour day you are entitled to take a break in the morning and in the afternoon," Kridel says. "It's a benefit to everyone, especially co-workers. You can get pretty crabby."[40]

Smokers Need Not Apply

While some companies have banned cigarette breaks, others have adopted an even harsher policy toward smokers: They refuse to hire them. Most large employers offer their full-time workers health insurance coverage, which pays for many of their medical bills. Health insurance is an important benefit for workers because

Studies show that employee cigarette breaks add up over time. The typical smoker spends about 240 hours a year on smoking breaks.

it protects them if they suffer catastrophic injuries or illnesses, which can cause them to be hospitalized for lengthy periods of time while undergoing expensive treatments. The cost of treating such illnesses or injuries can run into the hundreds of thousands of dollars, which many working people would be unable to afford.

The cost of this insurance is typically expensive, particularly if companies employ people who smoke. Lung cancer, heart disease, and other illnesses linked to smoking are regarded as catastrophic illnesses. By refusing to hire smokers, companies have found that their health insurance costs can be greatly reduced. Moreover, many smokers also have a negative effect on productivity because if they do contract a serious smoking-related illness, they could be out of work for weeks or months (assuming they survive their illnesses), forcing the company to hire replacement workers. Says John Banzhaf, executive director of Action on Smoking and Health, "Smoking is the biggest factor in controllable health care costs."[41]

> "We're trying to provide a workplace that is safe and healthy. We do care about the health of our [employees]."[42]
>
> — Ross McLerran, spokesperson for insurance company Humana.

Faced with such detrimental effects on their business, some employers have resolved to rid their staff of smokers. For years many companies have asked workers to make pledges that they would not smoke, but in recent years some employers have decided not to let smokers in the front door. In 2012, for example, Geisinger Health System, which operates several hospitals in Pennsylvania, announced that it would no longer hire smokers. Geisinger is not alone. The railroad Union Pacific has also informed job applicants they would not be hired if they smoke. One major employer that announced in 2011 it would no longer hire smokers is Humana, a health insurance company based in Arizona. "Cigarette smoking increases the risk of cancer and shortens life spans," Humana spokesperson Ross McLerran says. "We're trying to provide a workplace that is safe and healthy. We do care about the health of our [employees]."[42]

Random Drug Testing

Other companies have adopted even tougher policies. Alaska Airlines started the get-tough trend toward employee smoking when it announced in the mid-1980s that it would make job applicants undergo drug testing for nicotine, and if they tested positive they would not be hired. Weyco, a Michigan company that administers health insurance plans for small businesses, has gone a step further—its 200 employees must undergo random drug testing intended to detect nicotine in their bodies. Howard Weyers, the president of Weyco, is a former college football coach and an exercise fanatic. Weyers says he imposes drug testing on his workers because he is concerned about the health of his employees. Weyers conceived the idea for the tests after speaking with a client who informed him that he intends to ban smoking at his company. Says Weyers, "I'm with a client one day and he told me, 'We're going to stop hiring smokers.' And I said, 'You're kidding me.' I reacted just like everybody else did [and said] 'You can't do that.' Oh, yes you can."[43]

Civil libertarians have sided with the smokers, contending that Weyco and similar companies have no right to prohibit legal activities by their employees outside the workplace. Kary Moss, executive director of the Michigan chapter of the ACLU, says that if companies can ban smoking outside the workplace, they could feel further emboldened to ban other activities. Perhaps, she suggests, an employer would not want to hire a woman out of fear she would get pregnant and take leave, forcing the company to find a temporary replacement. Or, she says, employees who enjoy sunbathing may be barred from employment due to their exposure to the sun and the possibility of contracting skin cancer. "What's next?" she asks. "Sitting in the sun? Getting pregnant?"[44] Adds Lewis Maltby, president of the Princeton, New Jersey–based National Workrights Institute, "Once you cross the line and allow employers to control any type of behavior that's not related to job performance, there's no limit to the harm that can and will be done."[45]

"Once you cross the line and allow employers to control any type of behavior that's not related to job performance, there's no limit to the harm that can and will be done."[45]

— Lewis Maltby, president of the National Workrights Institute.

Cutting Costs

But employers defend their policies, insisting that their success is judged by their bottom lines. If companies find themselves becoming less profitable because they must spend more on health insurance or employees who have to take lengthy sick leaves, they are naturally going to look for ways to cut those costs. Says Susan Lessack, an attorney with Pepper Hamilton, a Philadelphia-based law firm that represents many corporate clients, "Employers are becoming increasingly aggressive about eliminating smoking in the workplace and trying to manage its attendant costs not only by imposing on-the-job bans but also by adopting policies that address employees' off-the-job behaviors."[46]

Employers may not like hiring smokers, but sometimes they have no choice. Companies that need to recruit manual laborers or other unskilled workers often find it difficult to recruit employees who do not smoke. It has long been an established fact that poor and uneducated people smoke in greater numbers than the educated and affluent. A 2008 poll by the Gallup Organization found that smokers account for 30 percent of workers who earn less than $6,000 a year and 34 percent of workers who earn between $6,000 and $12,000 a year. In contrast, just 13 percent of workers who earn more than $90,000 a year are smokers. The statistics mean that a lot of people who perform manual labor or similar unskilled tasks are smokers. Since such workers are often vital to a business, companies may have no choice but to hire them. "Some employment pools are high in smokers, such as those that draw from uneducated applicants," says Karen Chadwick, a professor at Thomas M. Cooley Law School in Ann Arbor, Michigan. "You are eliminating workers who have something to bring to the table."[47]

Defending Smokers

Job applicants who have been denied employment because of their smoking habits have appealed to state legislators for protection, and many lawmakers have responded. By 2012, 29 states as well as the District of Columbia adopted laws that protect off-duty employees from smoking bans imposed by their companies. These statutes are known as "lifestyle discrimination laws." Essentially, most of the laws say that employers cannot discriminate against workers who engage in legal activities while off the job. Since tobacco use by adults is legal, these laws protect smokers from discrimination at the workplace. According to the ACLU:

> Americans have long accepted that employers have a certain degree of control over what we do while at the workplace. But increasing numbers of employers are dangerously broadening the sphere of their control to include what employees do in their own homes. Many employers now refuse to hire people whose private lives are deemed "unhealthy." A few even fire current employees who don't change their

Charging Smokers More for Insurance

Employers forced to bear the high cost of providing health insurance to employees who smoke have started passing that cost on to their nicotine-addicted employees. Workers typically share in the cost of buying health insurance through payroll deductions. At many American companies, employees who smoke are finding their payroll deductions are growing larger than nonsmoking coworkers.

A 2011 study by Towers Watson, a New York City–based benefits consulting firm, found that 19 percent of the 248 companies it surveyed make their smoking employees pay more for health insurance—double the number that assessed the higher deductions in 2009. By 2013, the consultant predicted, the rate would double again.

One company that requires smoking employees to pay more for health insurance is Walmart, the huge retailer that employs 1.4 million people at its more than 4,400 stores in America. Walmart employees who smoke pay as much as $2,000 more a year for their health insurance than coworkers who do not smoke. "Tobacco users consume 25 percent more health care services than nontobacco users," says Greg Rossiter, a spokesperson for Walmart.

One Walmart employee affected by the hike is Bonnie Shoaf, 60, who says she does not intend to give up smoking. "This is drastic," she says. "There goes my food money. I don't have any choice, but I will have to pay for it."

Quoted in *Wall Street Journal*, "Walmart Trims Health Care Coverage for Some," October 21, 2011. http://online.wsj.com.

lifestyle to meet new company demands. The most common victims of this type of discrimination are smokers. . . .

The driving force behind this trend is economics. Health care costs for employers are increasing by at least 15 percent

> per year. . . . Although several factors contribute to these rising costs, the only factor employers have control over is their employees. With such an incentive, employers may well try to dominate every health related aspect of their employees' lives, including diet, exercise and sleep habits, and without protective legislation they will succeed.[48]

In many cases lifestyle discrimination laws are endorsed by antismoking activists who insist that smokers give up many of their rights because they willingly endanger their own health while also endangering the health of others by polluting the air with second-hand smoke. In addition, critics argue, the cost of a company's health insurance is shared by nonsmokers through the payroll deductions they contribute to the insurance plans. Says Radley Balko, a policy analyst for the Cato Institute, which advocates for civil liberties:

> Health insurance is essentially the distribution of risk. A large number of people pay into a pool, managed by the

The American Civil Liberties Union (ACLU) has fought attempts to prohibit employees from smoking cigarettes outside the workplace in their off hours. ACLU officials fear that such measures will embolden employers to seek control over other employee activities during nonworking hours.

> health insurance company. The company operates on the assumption that only a few of its customers will get sick enough to require more money out of the pool than what they pay in. The problem is that . . . high risk customers tend to pay the same or similar premiums as low-risk customers. So people who make good decisions about what they eat, how often they exercise, or what habits they take up, end up subsidizing people who make less-healthy decisions. It amounts to an incentive for unhealthy behavior.[49]

According to a 2011 report by the Kaiser Family Foundation, a California organization that studies trends in American medicine, the typical American employee contributes $4,100 a year to his or her health insurance plan—regardless of whether he or she is a smoker or nonsmoker. In other words, a nonsmoker contributes the same amount each year to his or her health insurance coverage as a smoker, even though it is likely that the smoker will require more health care than the nonsmoker.

Cracking Down on Loose Tobacco

Despite a few victories in the area of individual rights, most smokers know that the tide of public opinion is running against them. Many lawmakers and other government officials are dedicated to finding ways to chip away at smokers' access to cigarettes while heaping new taxes on cigarette sales. For example, in New York City police have cracked down on smokers who buy so-called "loose" tobacco so they can roll their own cigarettes. In the city, the high cost of cigarettes has prompted many smokers to buy tobacco by the bag because loose tobacco is taxed at a much lower rate than manufactured cigarettes.

The tax on loose tobacco is less because this type of tobacco is typically used for pipe smoking or for smokeless use. Although pipe tobacco and smokeless tobacco present their own health risks, they are not considered as deadly as cigarette tobacco. Moreover, there are far fewer pipe smokers and smokeless tobacco users than cigarette smokers.

As the taxes on cigarettes skyrocketed in New York, some

Banning Cigarette Sales in Pharmacies

For years smokers could count on finding cigarettes for sale at local pharmacies, but in recent years lawmakers have taken a dim view of permitting stores to sell cigarettes that otherwise provide prescription drugs meant to help keep people healthy. San Francisco became the first city to ban tobacco sales in pharmacies when the city council passed a measure in 2008 forcing the stores to remove the products from their shelves. "Pharmacies are places we go to get healthy," says New York State Assembly member Sam Hoyt, who proposed a statewide ban on pharmacy cigarette sales in 2009. "It just seems inappropriate that on the other hand, they sell something that kills."

By 2012 Hoyt was unable to muster enough votes in the legislature to enact the statewide ban, but elsewhere similar measures are moving forward. In late 2011 officials in Massachusetts said they would consider a statewide ban.

Todd Brown, executive director of the Massachusetts Independent Pharmacists Association, a trade organization representing about 150 pharmacies, says more than half of his group's members have already taken tobacco products off their shelves. Nevertheless, Brown insists that a statewide ban would have little impact on Massachusetts smokers. He says, "We have not seen any evidence that restricting sales at pharmacies reduces access, because people can go to the grocery store or gas station next door to get the products."

Quoted in *USA Today*, "Pressure Mounts for Pharmacies to Put Out Smokes," May 9, 2008, p. 1A.

Quoted in Kay Lazar, "Regulators Consider Ban on Tobacco Sales in Pharmacies," *Boston Globe*, November 10, 2011. www.bostonglobe.com.

entrepreneurs went into business specifically to sell cigarette tobacco by the bag. Typically, these stores also sell cigarette papers and provide machines that enable customers to roll their own cigarettes. In 2011 New York City authorities launched a crackdown, bringing civil lawsuits against Island Smokes, a company that operated two such stores in the city and had plans to open two more. Authorities charged that the owners of Island Smokes exploited a loophole in the city's tobacco sales law, treating bags of cigarette tobacco as though they were bags of pipe tobacco or smokeless tobacco. This loophole enabled them to sell cigarettes without adding on the high taxes they would otherwise have to charge. As such, Island Smokes was able to cut the normal price of a cigarette by half.

To settle the lawsuit, Island Smokes agreed to go out of business. Jonathan Behrins, an attorney for Island Smokes, says he believes his clients could have defended their way of doing business, but in the end they decided the cost of the court case would have been too expensive. "They researched the law through and through, and there's a gaping exception for pipe and loose tobacco," Behrins says. "[Island Smokes] saw the opportunity to make a niche out of it."[50] New York officials disagreed. Says Michael Cardozo, the city's corporate counsel, "The success of the lawsuit should serve as a reminder to others thinking of 'gimmicks' to skirt New York City's tough cigarette laws that the city will enforce those laws vigorously."[51]

Smokers Enjoy Few Rights

For smokers in New York and elsewhere, the crackdown on the roll-your-own stores represents yet another case of the government making it harder and more expensive for them to obtain and enjoy cigarettes. As for smoking activist Audrey Silk, she has come up with her own solution. Silk has cultivated a tobacco crop in her backyard—a perfectly legal crop, as long as she does not sell the tobacco. Silk grows tobacco for personal use only. She admits it takes a lot of work to cultivate and harvest the crop—and she also spends several hours a week sitting at her kitchen table and rolling her own cigarettes—but she has found a legal way to get as much tobacco as she needs and never pay a dime in taxes. "I'm in a situation a lot of people don't get to enjoy," Silk says. "I have my own house with my own backyard. . . . You can grow this crop anywhere."[52]

Although Silk and other activists insist that smokers do have rights, many legal scholars believe their rights are limited. Samantha

"There is no constitutional right to smoke."[54]

— Samantha K. Graff, author of a study on smokers' rights commissioned by the Tobacco Control Legal Consortium.

K. Graff, author of a study on smokers' rights, contends there is no precedent in American law that would provide smokers the protection they seek in the workplace or in other places where they believe they are the victims of discrimination. Graff's study was commissioned by the Minnesota-based advocacy group Tobacco Control Legal Consortium.

Graff points out that the Fourteenth Amendment to the Constitution contains an equal protection clause that ensures all Americans are treated the same under the law, regardless of their race, ethnicity, gender, or religious affiliation. She contends that smokers do not qualify for equal protection. Says Graff:

> Some people argue that smokers make up a category that deserves special protection against discriminatory laws that restrict their ability to smoke at a time and place of their choosing. However, smokers are not a specially protected group under the Constitution. . . . People are not born smokers and smoking, while addictive, is still a behavior that people can stop. Since smokers are not a specially protected group, a smoke-free law that "discriminates" against smokers will not violate the equal protection clause.[53]

Therefore, according to Graff, it would seem that smokers have little standing to complain about violations of their rights because, in reality, smokers do not enjoy many rights at all. "There is no constitutional right to smoke," says Graff. "If there were a legal justification for a special right to smoke, it would come from the US Constitution."[54]

Facts

- By 2012 the 21 states that still permitted employers to ban smokers from their workforce were Alabama, Alaska, Arizona, Arkansas, Delaware, Florida, Georgia, Hawaii, Idaho, Iowa, Kansas, Maryland, Massachusetts, Michigan, Nebraska, Ohio, Pennsylvania, Texas, Utah, Vermont, and Washington.
- A 2011 poll by the Gallup Organization reported that 36 percent of Americans who do not have health insurance smoke cigarettes, meaning that they will be responsible for 100 percent of the cost of their treatment if they contract a disease, including a smoking-related disease.
- All employees of the supermarket chain Whole Foods are given 20 percent discounts when they shop in the stores. Since 2010 employees who are nonsmokers have qualified for discounts that are as high as 30 percent.
- A 2011 poll by the Gallup Organization reported that 85 percent of Americans believe smokers should not be barred from employment because of their habit.
- The Pennsylvania Supreme Court ruled unanimously in 2010 that the town council of Ellwood City overstepped its authority when it banned police officers from smoking in police cruisers and using smokeless tobacco on the job.
- In 2011 a federal appeals court upheld the right of Armstrong County Memorial Hospital in Pennsylvania to ban cigarette breaks on hospital premises. A union representing hospital employees challenged the ban.
- In 2011 the Alaska Supreme Court upheld an ordinance adopted by the Juneau City Council that bans smoking in private clubs. The ban had been challenged by the Fraternal Order of Eagles, which contended its members should have the right to smoke on club premises.

CHAPTER FOUR

Are There Other Ways to Get People to Stop Smoking?

In the years following the 1964 surgeon general's report, Congress and the state governments imposed taxes on tobacco as well as restrictions on advertising and other measures to reduce people's access to cigarettes and limit the places where they could smoke. Other nations were not as quick to impose similar regulations. Although some European countries banned tobacco ads on TV soon after the surgeon general's report—Great Britain initiated its ban on TV ads in 1965—others reacted much more slowly. There would be no continent-wide ban on TV tobacco advertising in Europe until 1991.

Still, by then most European nations had adopted American-style get-tough policies on smoking: banning tobacco use in restaurants and taverns, imposing workplace restrictions, assessing high taxes on cigarette sales, and financing public health programs designed to convince people to give up their smoking habit. And yet, despite all these efforts, people in Europe still smoke cigarettes in large numbers. No place is this fact more evident than in the Netherlands, where 27 percent of adults smoke cigarettes—a rate that is a third higher than the American smoking rate of 20.6 percent. The percentage of smokers among the Dutch people is high even though the government spends nearly $4 million a year on antismoking programs in a country of just 16 million people.

In 2010 Dutch lawmakers looked at the results of their antismoking programs and decided they were not working. Rather than reassess their strategy, government officials decided to eliminate funding for antismoking programs. "There's no other country that's taking these backward steps," says Lies van Gennip, director of the Dutch national tobacco-control program. "I'm ashamed at what's happening here."[55] Van Gennip's agency is slated to lose all of its funding by 2013.

The Dutch government has not only eliminated funding for tobacco control programs but also has scaled back its antismoking laws, providing exemptions for many taverns so that patrons can smoke inside the establishments. "People are on their own, that's the message the government is giving out,"[56] says Savitri Ritoe, who runs a smoking cessation clinic in The Hague, a Dutch city. Government funding for Ritoe's clinic was completely eliminated in 2012.

An empty bar in Amsterdam, with a prominently displayed no-smoking sign (left), suggests public discontent over Dutch laws prohibiting cigarette smoking in bars and other similar establishments.

In 2010 Dutch lawmakers eliminated funding for antismoking programs and scaled back antismoking laws.

Discouraging Tobacco Use

Although lawmakers in the Netherlands acknowledge that their antismoking efforts have not worked, authorities in America are pressing ahead. In 2010 the US Department of Health and Human Services issued a long-range plan intended to reduce the American tobacco habit. The report urges the imposition of further restrictions on tobacco advertising and marketing as well as additional tax hikes. The report also emphasizes the need for governmental resources to help convince people that smoking is bad for them.

Government-sponsored measures designed to help smokers kick their habit and to prevent others from lighting their first cigarette are not new. Soon after the surgeon general's 1964 report, Congress created the National Clearinghouse for Smoking and Health (NCSH). The agency was charged with the responsibility of compiling facts about tobacco use in America as well as developing public health programs that would discourage smoking. Daniel Horn, a psychologist employed by the American Cancer Society, was selected as the agency's first director. (The agency was later merged into the CDC and renamed the Office on Smoking and Health).

Congress gave Horn's agency a budget of just $2 million a year, hardly enough to counter the massive pro-smoking campaign financed by the tobacco companies. Nevertheless, Horn's agency developed some early programs. For example, in 1966 the NCSH gave Valley State College in Northridge, California, $188,000 to conduct a study on smoking and athletic performance. The college used the money to test the athletic abilities of 200 student athletes, including 100 smokers and 100 nonsmokers. The NCSH used the study to convince student athletes that their endurance would suffer if they smoked. "A young man is more interested in smoking's influence on his ability to run track than the fact that he may die from cancer 40 years from now,"[57] said John Fodor, a Valley State professor who headed the study.

The small Valley State project was typical for the era. With little funding, the NCSH lacked the resources to organize a comprehensive national antismoking campaign. Still, Horn traveled the country, giving speeches on the dangers of smoking and calling on Americans to kick their habits. He singled out teachers, urging them to stop smoking so they could set good examples for their students. Horn contended that it was not good enough for teachers to simply refrain from smoking in front of their students. He suggested that when the door of the faculty lounge opens and a cloud of blue cigarette smoke drifts into the school hallway, students know very well who is smoking inside. "By providing the teachers with a hideout in which to smoke and failing to discuss the problem, we may be creating an environment favorable to cigarette smoking,"[58] Horn warned in a 1965 speech before the American Association of School Administrators.

Smoking Cessation and Prevention Programs

In the years since Horn's tiny agency funded the first public health programs to discourage smoking, the state and federal governments have dramatically bolstered their commitments to smoking cessation and prevention projects. In 2011 the US government provided nearly $165 million in grants to the states to help them finance antismoking programs. The states have also provided their own funding, raised through taxes they impose on tobacco sales, grants obtained through private foundations, and the ongoing payments they receive from the tobacco companies through the 1994 lawsuit settlement. In 2011 the states financed public health programs with more than $477 million drawn from these sources—in addition to the money they received from the federal treasury.

"By providing the teachers with a hideout in which to smoke and failing to discuss the problem, we may be creating an environment favorable to cigarette smoking."[58]

— David Horn, first head of the National Clearinghouse for Smoking and Health.

Many states dispense their antismoking funds to help finance the American Lung Association's "Freedom From Smoking" classes, which meet at hospitals, community centers, and college campuses to teach smokers how to gradually wean themselves off tobacco. Group leaders discuss changes in diet, the importance of exercise, and ways to manage stress that help smokers remain calm without feeling the need to reach for cigarettes. A virtual version of the program is also available online for Internet users. In addition,

Paying Smokers to Quit

In 2011 the federal and state governments spent nearly $650 million on smoking cessation and prevention programs—and yet more than 20 percent of American adults continue to smoke. According to a 2009 study by the University of Pennsylvania in Philadelphia, that money may be better spent if it is paid directly to the smokers.

Nearly 900 employees of the General Electric Company (GE) participated in the study. All were smokers who burned through more than a pack of cigarettes a day. The participants were divided into two groups. Both groups participated in smoking cessation programs, but members of one group were offered financial incentives that were as high as $750, depending on the length of time they abstained from smoking following the completion of their classes. Members of the other group received no financial incentives.

Eighteen months after the smoking classes ended, nearly 10 percent of the GE employees who received financial incentives remained smoke free. In the group that did not receive financial incentives, just 3.6 percent managed to remain smoke free. Asked why she quit smoking, GE employee Loretta Massie-Eaton said, "It was the satisfaction of sticking to the commitment and getting reimbursed for doing it."

Quoted in Robert Tomsho, "More Smokers Quit If Paid, Study Shows," *Wall Street Journal*, February 12, 2009, p. D1.

the program provides a hotline smokers can call when they feel cravings for cigarettes. On the hotline, a counselor provides moral support and attempts to help the caller deal with his or her crisis without the aid of a cigarette.

Mimi Long, an actress who lives in Los Angeles, started smoking at the age of 15. She finally gave up the habit 14 years later with the help of the Freedom From Smoking program. "You feel so alone, like no one else can understand your struggles on a moment-to-moment basis," she says. "You find out what you are experiencing is completely normal and that wanting to kill everyone in the room is a normal reaction to what you're dealing with. And [Freedom From Smoking] gives you ways to deal with that."[59]

Graphic Images on TV

Many antismoking projects make use of public service announcements (PSAs) on TV to drive home their messages. Authorities in Los Angeles established the Smoking: AnimAction program, which is conducted at 33 of the city's middle schools. At each school 140 students help animate a PSA that warns people of the dangers of smoking. The 33 cartoons are aired annually at an awards ceremony, where executives from Kids' WB!, Fox Kids, Cartoon Network, Toon Disney, and Disney Channel select the student-made PSAs that will be aired on their networks.

And in New York, the state health department sponsored a series of graphic TV commercials in 2010 intended to scare viewers into giving up their tobacco habit. In one PSA the gloved hand of a surgeon squeezes thick fatty deposits that have formed in the aorta of a 32-year-old smoker. The condition was caused by the smoker's cigarette habit. (The aorta is the main artery that leads away from the heart, providing blood to the body.) "Ads that are intense, graphic and emotionally arousing stick with viewers and motivate them to take action,"[60] says Maansi Bansal-Travers, a researcher at Roswell Park Cancer Institute in Buffalo, New York.

Antismoking Programs Feel the Ax

There are dozens of antismoking programs underway throughout the country, but in recent years there has been less money made available for smoking cessation and prevention projects. To balance their states' budget, legislatures have often been forced to cut back on spending—and antismoking programs often feel the ax of the budget cutter. According to the Campaign for Tobacco-Free Kids, federal aid for antismoking programs dropped by 28 percent between 2008 and 2011. Moreover, the organization found, state-financed spending in 2011 was nearly 10 percent less than in the year before. Thomas Frieden, director of the CDC, says he fears that if the state and federal governments continue to cut back on their smoking cessation and prevention programs, the smoking rate in America will start climbing upward. "There's a risk of a setback," Frieden says. "The data are very clear. The more we invest in tobacco control, the fewer people smoke, and that prevents illness, disability, deaths and health care costs."[61]

> "The data are very clear. The more we invest in tobacco control, the fewer people smoke, and that prevents illness, disability, deaths and health care costs."[61]
>
> — CDC director Thomas Frieden.

Indeed, despite the nearly $650 million in combined state and federal funds that have been spent to finance smoking cessation and prevention programs, critics believe authorities should be doing much more. Officials of the American Lung Association point out that while the federal and state governments are cutting back on antismoking programs, they are also becoming less likely to impose new taxes on tobacco products. "If states completely retreat, it will bring even more tragic human consequences across America," says Charles Connor, president of the American Lung Association. "A race to the bottom is not necessary when millions of lives are at stake."[62]

Can There Be a Safe Cigarette?

Even with the recent cutbacks in financing for smoking cessation and prevention programs, local, state, and federal governments still provide hundreds of millions of dollars for antismoking campaigns. None of that money would have to be spent if tobacco products could be made free of the toxic chemicals that shorten lives. However, despite decades of scientific research underwritten by the tobacco companies, all efforts to develop a safe cigarette have failed.

As far back as the 1950s, tobacco companies were coming to the same realization that the medical community had been drawing about smoking: that cigarettes presented serious health concerns. "Evidence is building up that heavy smoking contributes to lung cancer,"[63] wrote a Philip Morris scientist in 1958. The scientist went so far as to suggest that the company display the "intestinal fortitude to jump to the other side of the fence"[64] and admit that its products are harmful. Of course, the scientist said, to remain in business and outsell the competition, Philip Morris

Positive PSAs Work Best

The notion of scaring smokers into giving up their tobacco habits dates back to the 1960s, when the first antismoking PSAs started appearing on American TV. Typically, such PSAs depict cancer victims and others whose lives are endangered because of their cigarette habits.

Recent research suggests this may be an ill-advised strategy. A 2011 University of Missouri study found that smokers may be more inclined to heed the advice of a PSA when it is produced in a friendlier tone, emphasizing the positive aspects of life without tobacco. As part of the study, 49 smokers were invited to view a series of PSAs, some of which showed explicit health conditions related to smoking, and others that did not. As the participants watched the ads, researchers monitored their heart rates and facial reactions to the commercials.

The study found that when antitobacco PSAs try to scare people into quitting, the ads often backfire—causing people to become defensive about their habits. When people see these ads, the study says, they find them so disgusting that they stop paying attention. Says Paul Bolls, one of the lead researchers of the study, "Simply trying to encourage smokers to quit by exposing them to combined threatening and disgusting visual images is not an effective way to change attitudes and behaviors. . . . That kind of communication will usually result in a defensive avoidance response where the smoker will try to avoid the disgusting images, not the cigarettes."

Quoted in ScienceDaily, "Extreme Negative Anti-Smoking Ads Can Backfire, Experts Find," August 22, 2011. www.sciencedaily.com.

would have to develop a safe cigarette—one that would not harm people's health.

Although Philip Morris executives elected to publicly maintain that cigarette smoking is not harmful, they nevertheless pursued research into developing a safe cigarette. For decades Philip Morris as well as other tobacco companies poured millions of dollars into scientific research, attempting to develop a cigarette that would not cause cancer, emphysema, or any of the other ill effects of smoking. Over the years, they added filters to cigarettes, tinkered with the ingredients, attempted to develop synthetic substitutes for tobacco—once even trying to replace tobacco with wood pulp—and added substances they hoped would neutralize the toxic effects of the chemicals in cigarette smoke. All of these efforts failed.

The Myth of the Light Cigarette

Although tobacco companies may have failed to develop safe cigarettes, starting in the 1960s they did introduce to consumers so-called light cigarettes, which contain less tar than other cigarettes. Tobacco companies advertised light cigarettes as safer because low-tar cigarettes meant the smoker would inhale fewer carcinogenic elements found in cigarette smoke. For some 40 years, tobacco companies marketed certain brands of cigarettes labeled as "lights," implying that smoking Marlboro Lights or Newport Lights, for example, meant the smoker inhaled less tar and other noxious ingredients.

It was all a myth. In 2007 hearings before a congressional committee headed by US Senator Frank Lautenberg of New Jersey, it was determined that light cigarettes were just as deadly as any other type of cigarette. In fact, they could be even more hazardous to the health of smokers, according to Allan M. Brandt, a Harvard University history of medicine professor.

It was true, the cigarettes did contain less tar—but physicians questioned whether even a reduced-tar cigarette was safe to smoke. Moreover, studies found, with less tar in the cigarette, the smoker received less satisfaction from each draw of smoke. Therefore, to obtain satisfaction from the smoking experience, smokers of light

cigarettes were taking deeper and more frequent draws on their cigarettes and likely smoking more cigarettes as well. Says Brandt:

> Smokers who use a reduced-tar product, such as light cigarettes, compensate by taking larger puffs, thus drawing more deeply into their lungs the smoke of those products. So it may well be that some of these "light" products are a greater danger than the regular cigarettes. The industry, however, has . . . been allowed to market them as less dangerous to public health. . . .What Lautenberg's hearings really make clear is that the industry has explicitly understood this for many years and deceptively marketed this product. So smokers who otherwise might have quit thought they were reducing their risks by buying these cigarettes—in vain. The tobacco industry has for at least 40 years worked hard to mislead the American public about the relative safety of their products.[65]

Light cigarettes such as Marlboro Lights were touted by tobacco companies as a healthier alternative to regular cigarettes. Scientific research has shown this claim to be false; light cigarettes are actually more hazardous to a smoker's health.

Outlawing Light Cigarettes

The Senate committee concluded that light cigarettes were not safer than other cigarettes and, instead, were probably more dangerous. Later, when Congress provided the FDA with more authority over the tobacco industry, one of the agency's first actions was to outlaw the marketing of tobacco products as "light" cigarettes. Starting in 2010 cigarette companies could no longer advertise light cigarettes as safer than other cigarettes. Additionally, they were specifically barred from marketing cigarettes using such words as *light*, *mild*, *medium*, or *low* in their advertisements.

"Smokers who use a reduced-tar product, such as light cigarettes, compensate by taking larger puffs, thus drawing more deeply into their lungs the smoke of those products."[65]

— Allan M. Brandt, history of medicine professor at Harvard University.

The tobacco industry responded to the new FDA rule by keeping the low-tar cigarettes on the market while changing their marketing strategies and packaging. Marlboro Lights, for example, were renamed Marlboro Golds and marketed in gold-colored packs. Newport Lights were rebranded as Newport Menthol Golds. After these cigarettes hit the market, the New York City Health Department responded by airing a series of PSAs on TV. "Don't be fooled," one ad says. "All cigarettes contain the same poisons that make you sick and kill you."[66]

But while the FDA ban is intended to better inform the public about the deadly contents of all cigarettes, it does not seem to have made much difference: Consumers still want their light cigarettes. Longtime smoker Joe McKenna, a teacher from Pearl River, New York, told a reporter that he has been smoking Newport Light 100s for years (a 100 cigarette is 100 millimeters in length, slightly longer than the average cigarette) and does not intend to stop smoking his favorite brand simply because the FDA has made the company change the name, packaging, and marketing for the cigarette. "I'll ask for Newport Light 100s and I'll let them decipher it," McKenna explains. "It's just kind of ridiculous in the sense that you [already] know they're harmful for you."[67]

The E-Cigarette

Meanwhile, despite the FDA's contention that there is no such thing as a safe cigarette, researchers are still trying to develop a product that people can smoke without fear of contracting cancer and other smoking-related illnesses. Electronic cigarettes, or e-cigarettes, first went on the market in 2007. Developed by a Chinese inventor, Hon Lik, they are battery-powered cylinders that look like cigarettes. Inside is a vaporizing device that delivers a puff of mist to the smoker. (Using an e-cigarette is not known as smoking, but rather as "vaping.")

Although the mist contains no tar, it does contain nicotine and/or other chemicals that provide the smoker with the drug that he or she craves. To give the user a semblance of the smoking experience, the e-cigarette includes a tiny light at the end of the cylinder that glows when the smoker inhales, mimicking the glow of burning tobacco in a real cigarette.

Since e-cigarettes were first introduced, a number of manufacturers have released their own versions. Some e-cigarettes provide fruity flavors and colors. Critics worry that young people will be drawn to e-cigarettes, believing them to be safe but becoming addicted to nicotine—which would then lead teenagers to smoke real cigarettes. Other e-cigarettes are shaped like cigars or pipes, whereas others do not look like smoking products at all—some resemble computer flash drives. "E-cigarettes are often sold as safe, which is probably not true," says Prue Talbot, a toxicologist for the University of California–Riverside. "They may not be as dangerous as real cigarettes, but on the other hand, they could be. We just don't know."[68]

Few Regulations on E-cigarettes

In 2009 the FDA analyzed a number of e-cigarettes on the market, finding that the mist inhaled by smokers does contain some Cancer-causing chemicals—including diethylene glycol, an ingredient commonly found in antifreeze. The FDA declared that e-cigarettes are drug-delivery devices and announced intentions to ban them, but manufacturers of e-cigarettes challenged the FDA and won a court order preventing the ban. Following the ruling of the court, the FDA said it intends to perform additional research and develop regulations for the marketing of e-cigarettes.

Meanwhile, by 2012 few states had adopted regulations re-

Battery-powered e-cigarettes, such as the one pictured here, deliver a puff of nicotine-infused mist. Critics suspect they are just as dangerous as regular cigarettes but, to date, little research has been done on them.

garding e-cigarettes. Among those that have are New Jersey, which banned sales of e-cigarettes to people under the age of 19. Some locales, such as the Tacoma–Pierce County, Washington, have adopted ordinances regulating e-cigarettes. In 2011 the entity's board of health voted unanimously to ban sales of e-cigarettes to people under 18 but to permit adults to smoke e-cigarettes in bars and private places of employment, as long as the employers permit them. The vote by the board illustrates that, at this point, officials still do not have enough information about e-cigarettes to determine whether they are as harmful as tobacco products.

Before the board enacted its regulations, 17 people spoke before the panel—some arguing to permit use of e-cigarettes, others arguing to ban them. JoAnne Barkley of Spanaway, Washington, smoked cigarettes for 40 years and finally turned to e-cigarettes to help her kick the tobacco habit. "This e-cigarette has been the only thing I've tried that has helped me achieve my goal," Barkley says. "It's helping people. Don't take this away from us."[69] But Leonard Sanderson of Milton, Washington, disagrees. He says, "It's too bad electronic cigarettes are being marketed as something that's not a danger, because it really is."[70]

> "This e-cigarette has been the only thing I've tried that has helped me achieve my goal. It's helping people. Don't take this away from us."[69]
>
> — JoAnne Barkley, an e-cigarette smoker from Spanaway, Washington.

As regulators wrestle with the issue of whether e-cigarettes are as harmful as real cigarettes, they hope smokers and nonsmokers continue to pay attention to the PSAs that are on TV. Antismoking activists believe the messages can be effective, whether they are the benign messages produced by the schoolchildren of Los Angeles or the harsh images of diseased tissue that appear on TV screens in New York. Moreover, antismoking activists believe they have scored a victory by proving that "light" cigarettes are a myth and, in fact, may be more dangerous than other cigarettes. And even though governments are providing less money for smoking cessation and prevention campaigns than they have in the past, American officials know that the programs do work—a fact that government leaders in the Netherlands may eventually find out for themselves.

Facts

- The states spending the most on smoking cessation and prevention programs in 2011 were California ($70 million) and Florida ($62 million). The states that spent the least that year were Nevada and New Hampshire, neither of which budgeted state funds for smoking cessation and prevention.
- New York State budgeted $41 million for antismoking programs in 2011, about half of what the state spent in 2008. Even so, from 2008 through 2011, the state's adult smoking rate dropped from 16.8 percent to 15.5 percent, according to the New York State Department of Health.
- Philadelphia used a federal grant in 2010 to buy 4,500 nicotine patches offering them free to any smoker on request. The program, which is valued at $400 per smoker, also includes telephone counseling. A nicotine patch adheres to an arm slowly releasing nicotine, satisfying the smoker's craving without the need to inhale toxic chemicals.
- Colorado spent $6.7 million on antismoking programs in 2011, all of it financed by the state's share of the $246 billion tobacco settlement. For the first time since 2004, Colorado lawmakers promised in 2012 to add money raised by the state's cigarette tax to smoking cessation and prevention programs.
- The Netherlands made plans to eliminate its national antismoking campaign in 2013 despite the fact that the country's lung cancer rate is the fifth highest among the countries of Europe. Among the Dutch, 50 out of 100,000 people suffer from lung cancer, according to the World Health Organization. Among European countries, only Belgium, Denmark, Poland, and Hungary have higher rates of lung cancer.

CHAPTER FIVE

Would a Comprehensive Smoking Ban Be Effective?

The tiny nation of Bhutan is located in the Himalayan mountains, bordered on the north by China and on the south by India. Just 700,000 people live in the country, which is nestled 24,500 feet (7,468m) above sea level. The Bhutanese are ruled by a king, Jigme Singye Wangchuk, who nevertheless gives his subjects a voice in their government by permitting an elected parliament to enact laws. Since 2005 the parliament in the Asian nation has adopted a series of measures that have severely limited access by the Bhutanese people to cigarettes.

The Bhutanese parliament has not enacted an outright ban on tobacco products, but lawmakers have made sales of cigarettes within the country illegal—shopkeepers who sell cigarettes can be sentenced to prison terms for as long as five years. Each day, police patrol the neighborhoods of Bhutan's capital, Thimphu, and other cities, accompanied by dogs trained to sniff out tobacco.

No tobacco is grown in Bhutan. The only way for a smoker to obtain cigarettes is to buy them by mail order, but even that procedure is severely limited—smokers are allowed to purchase just 200 cigarettes a month. Moreover, the parliament has assessed high taxes on cigarette imports that have increased the price of a pack by 200 percent. Lawmakers have also outlawed smoking everywhere in the country with the exception of inside smokers' own homes. "We want no pollution and good health for our citizens,"[71] a Bhutanese official told a reporter.

It is estimated that less than 1 percent of the population of Bhutan are smokers. Due to the parliament's actions, many citizens of Bhutan believe the day is nearing when the country will be completely smoke free. "If you can't get it, you can't smoke it,"[72] shrugs Tshewang Dendup, who picked up the smoking habit while attending college in California. Dendup says he smokes far fewer cigarettes than he did before the tough laws on smoking were enacted.

Criminal Organizations

Bhutan may have succeeded in all but banning smoking, but experts doubt that such draconian antismoking laws would succeed elsewhere—particularly in America. In America, leaders of the antismoking movement know that a complete ban on smoking, or even a near-ban similar to what has been enacted in Bhutan, is unlikely to occur.

Officials fear that even if Congress were to adopt an outright ban on smoking, the law would never be enforceable. They predict that a ban on cigarettes would lead to a repeat of the Prohibition era—the time in American society from 1919 to 1933 when alcoholic beverages were made illegal by the Eighteenth Amendment to the US Constitution. The national ban on alcohol manufacturing and sales led to the emergence of vast criminal organizations that provided millions of Americans with alcoholic beverages.

> "If you can't get it, you can't smoke it."[72]
>
> — Bhutanese smoker Tshewang Dendup.

Throughout Prohibition, politicians and law enforcement officers were easily corrupted by bootleggers, who built their empires through strong-arm tactics that often included murder. In a 2011 article for the *New England Journal of Medicine*, antismoking advocates James Colgrove, Ronald Bayer, and Kathleen Bachynski write, "Most health professionals agree that an outright prohibition on the sale of cigarettes would be unfeasible and would lead to unwanted consequences such as black markets and the crime that accompanies them."[73]

Cigarette Smuggling in America

Experts worry about the consequences of an outright ban because cigarette smuggling is already a crime that occurs frequently in America. Typically, smugglers buy cartons of cigarettes in states where the taxes are low, then transport them to states that assess high taxes on tobacco sales. A typical case occurred in 2011 when police stopped a car on Interstate 95, a major East Coast highway, and found 12 cases of cigarettes in the vehicle.

The 12 cases held 3,600 packs of cigarettes. The suspect was alleged to have bought them in Virginia, where the state tax on cigarettes is 30 cents per pack, and then headed to New York to sell them, where the state tax on a pack of cigarettes is $4.25. Obviously, the smuggler hoped to turn a profit by selling the cigarettes

The Himalayan nation of Bhutan, ruled by King Jigme Singye Wangchuk (pictured), has outlawed the sale of cigarettes. The penalty for selling cigarettes, up to five years in prison, has contributed to a dramatic decrease in smoking in Bhutan but few think such a ban would succeed in the United States.

The Highest Smoking Rates on Earth

Many countries, mostly in Africa and Asia, have virtually no laws regulating tobacco products. Not surprisingly, these countries have some of the heaviest tobacco-use rates in the world. According to a 2007 study by *Forbes* magazine, tobacco use is heaviest in the country of Nauru, a tiny island nation of about 13,500 people located about 2,000 miles (3,219km) northeast of Australia. According to *Forbes*, 54 percent of the adult population of Nauru are smokers.

Other countries with heavy smoking rates are the African nations of Guinea (52 percent), Namibia (50 percent), and Kenya (49 percent). These countries not only have the world's highest smoking rates but also some of the world's worst health care. "In Africa, these health care systems don't exist, at least not in the form we're used to," says Tom Glynn, director of International Cancer Control for the American Cancer Society.

These same countries also share some of the lowest rates of life expectancy on the planet. In Namibia the life expectancy is 52, whereas the average Guinean can expect to live to be 58. The average life expectancy in Kenya is 63; in Nauru it is 65. In contrast, the average life expectancy in America is 78.

Quoted in Tom Van Riper, "The World's Heaviest-Smoking Countries," *Forbes*, December 4, 2007. www.forbes.com.

to buyers anxious to avoid paying the high New York State tax rate. "This is becoming the new organized crime, the new Prohibition," says Rich Marianos, an agent for the Bureau of Alcohol, Tobacco and Firearms (ATF), the federal law enforcement agency that tracks down cigarette smugglers. "Every day we see more and more criminal organizations utilizing illegal cigarettes to facilitate their operations."[74]

ATF officials estimate that a carload of smuggled cigarette cartons can net the smuggler a profit of at least $30,000. And a carload of smuggled cigarettes is regarded as a relatively small haul. ATF agents have chased down tractor-trailers carrying 800 cases or more of smuggled cigarettes. Of course, when people buy smuggled cigarettes, they are not paying the rightful taxes imposed on the tobacco products. According to Philip Awe, director of the tobacco division of the ATF, cigarette smuggling costs governments at least $5 billion a year in lost revenue. "It's a big business and it's getting horribly bigger,"[75] says Paul Carey III, coordinator of enforcement for the Northern Virginia Cigarette Tax Board, which collects Virginia's cigarette tax.

Some cigarette smugglers have set up Internet sites that enable people to buy untaxed cigarettes, which are shipped to them through the US mail. Congress responded to the growing threat of cigarette smuggling in 2009 by passing the Prevent All Cigarette Trafficking Act, or PACT. Under the terms of the new law, federal regulators tightened the rules that require tobacco companies and their shippers to report the quantities of cigarette packs they transport. The new rules make it harder for retailers to mix in smuggled cigarettes with stocks of cigarettes they have bought legally. During an ATF inspection, the retailer would be asked to show records of how the cigarettes were obtained. Also, the law makes it mandatory that each carton containing cigarettes be clearly marked to indicate that it contains cigarettes. Moreover, PACT made it illegal to ship cigarettes through the US Postal Service. Convicted cigarette smugglers face up to three years in federal prison. In addition, the law imposes fines on smugglers of as much as $10,000 as well as 2 percent of the value of the smuggled cigarettes found in their possession.

Subsidizing Tobacco Farmers

Cigarette smuggling may be hurting the economies of many states, denying them billions of dollars in lost tax revenue, but an outright ban on cigarette sales would have a much more devastating impact on the American economy. Outlawing cigarettes would immediately throw some 660,000 Americans out of work, according to a 2004 report by the North Carolina Department of Agriculture.

That estimate includes the number of people who are employed in the fields by the nation's more than 16,000 tobacco farms or in the factories, warehouses, and corporate offices of cigarette manufacturers. Others are employed in businesses that rely on the tobacco trade, including wholesalers, warehousers, retailers, packagers, trucking companies, and other shippers, among other businesses. According to the CDC, tobacco companies earn about $84 billion a year on cigarette sales as well as another $6 billion on the sales of cigars, pipe tobacco, and smokeless tobacco. A significant portion of that income goes into the paychecks of the tobacco industry's workers and is therefore funneled back into the American economy.

Tobacco has a long history of cultivation in America dating back to the days of the Jamestown colony. During the Great Depression of the 1930s, as farmers everywhere struggled, Congress provided subsidies for the agricultural industry—including growers of tobacco. Administered by the US Department of Agriculture (USDA), the program set quotas on how much tobacco farmers could grow and how many acres could be devoted to tobacco cultivation. The quotas created demand, which helped farmers sell their crops at a profit. Moreover, farmers could also receive low-interest loans from the USDA to help them plant new crops.

Protector of the Tobacco Industry

When the USDA provided a low-interest loan for a tobacco grower, it meant that taxpayers made up the difference between the true interest rate and the rate the farmer was required to pay. Therefore, starting in 1933 American taxpayers helped pay for the cultivation of a crop that would eventually be found to be responsible for the deaths of millions of Americans. The tobacco subsidy law stayed on the books well after the 1964 surgeon general's report, thanks to the efforts of powerful lawmakers in Washington, DC, who represented tobacco-growing states and fiercely defended the laws that favored their constituents.

Perhaps the most powerful protector of the tobacco industry

was Jesse Helms of North Carolina, who represented his state in the US Senate for 30 years. "You have politicians in this area who genuinely have the farmer's interests in hand," a tobacco warehouse owner told author Peter Benson. "Jesse Helms, for example, was thought of as a tobacco god. In the 1980s, I was at farm meetings where Jesse Helms walked in and it was as if Jesus had walked into the life of the American tobacco farmer. He was the great champion of their product."[76]

> "In the 1980s, I was at farm meetings where Jesse Helms walked in and it was as if Jesus had walked into the life of the American tobacco farmer. He was the great champion of their product."[76]
>
> — North Carolina tobacco warehouse owner.

The administration of President Ronald Reagan ended the low-interest loan program for tobacco growers in 1981—but not before American taxpayers had provided some $591 million in assistance to the farmers since the years of the Great Depression. However, the quota system, which kept prices high for consumers and guaranteed the tobacco industry would remain healthy, stayed in place.

Tobacco Rebounds

Helms retired from the Senate in 2003 at the age of 81. A year later, with tobacco farmers lacking their most ardent defender in Washington, Congress passed the Tobacco Transition Program, which phased out the quota system over a 5-year period. The legislation also required tobacco companies to pay $10 billion to tobacco farmers over a 10-year period to help them through the transition period. The authors of the legislation hoped many of the farmers would use the money to plant crops other than tobacco.

Many American tobacco farmers were convinced that despite the assistance they would receive from tobacco companies, the phaseout of their subsidies would severely harm their businesses. After all, in the years between the release of the 1964 surgeon general's report and the commencement of the transition program, cigarette use by Americans had been reduced by nearly half. Without their subsidies, many farmers expected to face bankruptcy. "The little guys won't survive this," predicted tobacco farmer Billy Massengill, tender of an 8-acre (3.24ha) farm in Smithfield, North Carolina. "Unfortunately, I'm one of the little guys."[77]

At first many farmers did get out of the tobacco business. According to a report by the Library of Congress, in 1998 some 718,000 farm acres (290,564ha) in America were devoted to tobacco crops. By 2005, the first year after the phaseout of the subsidies commenced, tobacco acreage had declined to just 297,000 acres (120,192ha).

"If somebody told me seven or eight years ago that I'd be growing tobacco today, I'd say they were crazy."[78]

— Illinois farmer Martin Ray Barbre.

However, the crop would soon rebound. It was true that American demand had steadily fallen since the 1960s, but tobacco companies were finding new markets for their products—particularly in China, Russia, and other countries that were anxious to open trade with the West. During the five-year phaseout period, farmers started returning to tobacco. By 2010 more than 337,000 acres (136,379ha) were devoted to growing tobacco on American soil. Illinois farmer Martin Ray Barbre gave up growing corn for tobacco. "If somebody told me seven or eight years ago that I'd be growing tobacco today, I'd say they were crazy," he says. "There's no way corn can [compete with tobacco]. There's too much money in tobacco."[78]

Economic Punch of Smoking Bans

A comprehensive ban on tobacco would affect not only the livelihoods of farmers and others who make their livings growing the crop and turning the leaves into cigarettes but other business owners as well. When states started banning smoking in taverns, the economic punch was felt mostly by the tavern owners. It seemed that if many of their customers could not light cigarettes while enjoying their cocktails or beers, they preferred to do their drinking at home. "When someone builds a business with a clientele that smokes, they should be able to go in there and smoke,"[79] insists Mike Reid, owner of a wine bar in Casper, Wyoming.

In Wyoming, lawmakers proposed a smoking ban on bars in 2009 but dropped their plans after bar owners complained. Meanwhile, in New Jersey lawmakers adopted a smoking ban for bars and other indoor places in 2006 but exempted the 11 casinos in the resort town of Atlantic City after 5 of the casinos said they would go bankrupt if gamblers could not smoke. The casinos are

Atlantic City's biggest employers; collectively they provide more than 37,000 jobs. In the end lawmakers were able to reach a compromise, permitting the casinos to set aside 25 percent of their gambling floor space for smokers. "A 100 percent smoking ban would be catastrophic,"[80] says Mark Juliano, chief executive officer of Trump Entertainment Resorts, which operates three casinos in Atlantic City.

A North Carolina farmer inspects his tobacco plants. For years, US tobacco farmers received low-interest loans and other government assistance that kept the tobacco industry healthy. Congressional action in the past decade has been aimed at getting farmers to transition to other crops.

Antismoking activists reacted harshly to these arguments, criticizing local governments that have backtracked on their smoking restrictions after hearing complaints from business owners. Stanton Glantz, director of the Center for Tobacco Control Research and Education at the University of California San Francisco, says people have continued to shop and enjoy movies and plays even though smoking has been banned in stores and theaters for decades. Says Glantz, "This whole economic argument is hogwash."[81]

New Warning Labels

The tobacco industry contends that it provides a significant boost to the American economy, but Glantz and other critics are quick to point out the economic harm caused by smoking. According to the CDC, smoking-related illnesses add $96 billion a year to the cost of American health care. Moreover, American companies lose $97 billion a year in production due to employees whose smoking habits have made them ill. In terms of human life, the CDC reports that 443,000 Americans die each year from smoking-related illnesses; 49,000 of those deaths are caused by secondhand smoke.

These statistics suggest why efforts by antismoking activists continue. They have long realized they will probably never win a comprehensive ban on smoking. Given the types of crime that such a ban would likely prompt, many do not even feel a comprehensive ban is a good idea. Still, antismoking activists continue to push lawmakers and other government officials for new ways to remind people that smoking is bad for them.

> "When someone builds a business with a clientele that smokes, they should be able to go in there and smoke."[79]
>
> — Mike Reid, owner of a wine bar in Casper, Wyoming.

Under an FDA mandate, starting in 2012 new warning labels were supposed to have appeared on cigarette packs. These labels represented a stark departure from the familiar labels found on cigarette packs, which since 1966 had been composed entirely of text. The new labels were designed to include graphic and colorful images of the health consequences of smoking, including a human lung infested with cancer cells; a display of human gums and teeth affected by mouth cancer; a patient strapped to an apparatus feeding him oxygen; a corpse of a cancer victim, and similar stark images. "We want to make a difference and help people who are smoking stop smoking and discourage people who haven't taken up the habit yet,"[82] FDA commissioner Margaret Hamburg says. In past years the labels were printed on the sides of the packs, as well as in print advertising for cigarette brands. Under the new FDA rules, the warning labels and photos would appear on the top half of the front of the pack, above the cigarette brand name and logo.

Tobacco Smuggling and Terrorism

A total ban on cigarette sales in America could help fuel terrorism, because law enforcement agencies have determined that profits from cigarette smuggling are often funneled to terrorist cells in the Middle East and elsewhere. In 2002, for example, a federal jury convicted Mohammad Hammoud of heading a ring that earned nearly $8 million by selling cigarettes in Michigan that had been smuggled out of North Carolina. During his trial, prosecutors presented evidence indicating that Hammoud funneled the profits to Hezbollah, a terrorist group based in Lebanon. Hammoud was sentenced to life in prison.

Since then, other cigarette smuggling cases have been linked to terrorist groups such as the Real Irish Republican Army, the Kurdistan Workers' Party, the Fuerzas Armadas Revolucionarias de Colombia (in English, the Revolutionary Armed Forces of Colombia), and al Qaeda, the group responsible for the 2001 attacks on New York City and Washington, DC.

Says US Senator Herb Kohl of Wisconsin, who introduced the legislation creating the Prevent All Cigarette Trafficking Act, "Cutting off financial support to terrorist groups is an integral part of protecting this country against future attacks. We can no longer continue to let terrorist organizations exploit weaknesses in our tobacco laws to generate significant amounts of money. The cost of doing nothing is too great."

Office of Senator Herb Kohl, "Kohl Sponsors Bill to Prevent Black Market Cigarette Smuggling," press release, May 21, 2009. www.kohl.senate.gov.

In 2012 the tobacco companies convinced a federal judge to block the new warning labels. US District Judge Richard J. Leon found that the labels violate the tobacco companies' right to free speech. The judge ruled that compelling tobacco companies to print the images on the packs equated to government-mandated speech, a violation of the First Amendment to the US Constitution. "It's basically rooted in the notion that compelled speech by the government is presumptively unconstitutional," says Floyd Abrams, an attorney who represents Lorillard Tobacco. "The only exception that could fit here is the one which says that the government can require warnings to be placed on products including tobacco products, but that the warnings must be factual and uncontroversial in nature."[83] Nevertheless, the US Department of Justice indicated it plans to appeal Leon's ruling to a higher court.

Today's Smokers

The delay in the implementation of the new warning labels represents a rare victory for the tobacco industry. Since the issuance of the surgeon general's report in 1964, the American market for tobacco has suffered a steady decline, with most Americans siding with the forces of the antitobacco movement. For example, in 2001 a poll by the Gallup Organization found that just 20 percent of Americans believe smoking should be prohibited in all public places, such as parks and beaches. In 2011 Gallup polled again on the question and found that 59 percent, a clear majority, support a ban on smoking in all public places.

> *"This whole economic argument [in support of smoking] is hogwash."*[81]
>
> — Stanton Glantz, director of the Center for Tobacco Control Research and Education at the University of California–San Francisco.

Moreover, in the new poll there was even an uptick in the number of people who believe that smoking should be completely outlawed. In 2001, 14 percent of the respondents supported a total ban on smoking in America. In 2011 that number rose slightly, to 19 percent. This means that although 1 in 5 Americans continue to smoke, a virtually equal number believe smoking should be outlawed.

Although a comprehensive ban on tobacco is unlikely to occur, smoking is a much different experience than it was a half century ago. Back in the 1950s and 1960s, the advertising campaigns of tobacco companies successfully convinced Americans that smoking was the habit of sophisticated people, high-powered executives, rugged cowboys, and hip young people. In the years since the truth about tobacco emerged, the people who have continued to smoke are those who are addicted to cigarettes and lack the will to quit. Those smokers as well as others are able to afford the high taxes on the cigarettes they buy, endure the sad images of cancer victims they see on televised PSAs and manage to find the few remaining places in public where the law still allows them to light up.

Facts

- In 2011 a committee of legislators in Bhutan proposed increasing the maximum number of cigarettes a citizen could import each month from 200 to 300. Members of the country's full parliament voted down the proposal.

- The smoking rate in China is 30 percent, according to a 2012 poll by the Gallup Organization. Gallup estimated that 300 million Chinese are smokers—a number that comes close to equaling the entire population of America.

- A national ban on tobacco use would have the biggest economic impact on North Carolina, where tobacco farmers harvested 352 million pounds (159.7 million kg) of tobacco in 2010, according to the Agricultural Marketing Resource Center in Ames, Iowa. Kentucky ranked second in tobacco production in 2010; farmers in that state harvested 181 million pounds (82.1 million kg) of tobacco.

- In 2010 tobacco was harvested in 23 states, according to the Agricultural Marketing Resource Center. Tobacco is the eighth-highest-valued field crop in America, following corn, soybeans, hay, wheat, cotton, potatoes, and rice.

Source Notes

Introduction: Clearing the Air in New York City

1. Quoted in Javier C. Hernandez, "Smoking Ban for Beaches and Parks Is Approved," *New York Times*, February 3, 2011, p. A22.
2. Quoted in Ron Scherer, "New York Poised to Ban Smoking in Central Park, Times Square," *Christian Science Monitor*, February 3, 2011, p. 1.
3. Quoted in Michael B. Siegel, "A Smoking Ban Too Far," *New York Times*, May 6, 2011, p. A25.
4. Quoted in Hernandez, "Smoking Ban for Beaches and Parks Is Approved," p. A22.
5. Quoted in Hernandez, "Smoking Ban for Beaches and Parks Is Approved," p. A22.
6. Quoted in Hernandez, "Smoking Ban for Beaches and Parks Is Approved," p. A22.
7. Siegel, "A Smoking Ban Too Far," p. A25.
8. Quoted in Scherer, "New York Poised to Ban Smoking in Central Park, Times Square," p. 1.

Chapter One: What Are the Origins of the Smoking Ban Controversy?

9. Quoted in Edward M. Brecher, *The Consumers Union Report on Licit and Illicit Drugs*. Mount Vernon, NY: Consumers Union, 1972, p. 230.
10. Quoted in Iain Gately, *Tobacco: A Cultural History of How an Exotic Plant Seduced Civilization*. New York: Grove, 2001, p. 23.
11. Quoted in Gately, *Tobacco*, p. 24.
12. Quoted in Gately, *Tobacco*, p. 33.
13. Quoted in Tony Williams, *The Jamestown Experiment: The Remarkable Story of the Enterprising Colony and the Unexpected Results That Shaped America*. Naperville, IL: Sourcebooks, 2011, p. 242.
14. Quoted in Gately, *Tobacco*, p. 234.
15. Quoted in Walter Sullivan, "Cigarettes Peril Health, US Report Concludes; 'Remedial Action' Urged," *New York Times*, January 12, 1964, p. 65.

16. Quoted in Laury Oaks, *Smoking and Pregnancy: The Politics of Fetal Protection*. New Brunswick, NJ: Rutgers University Press, 2001, p. 65.

17. US Centers for Disease Control and Prevention, "Highlights: Warning Labels," August 9, 2000. www.cdc.gov.

18. US Centers for Disease Control and Prevention, "Highlights: Warning Labels."

19. Quoted in Derrick Z. Jackson, "Worcester Fights Smoking, Sign by Sign," *Boston Globe*, June 25, 2011. www.boston.com.

Chapter Two: Have Bans on Youth Cigarette Sales Affected Teen Smoking Rates?

20. Quoted in Patrick J. Murphy, "Teen Smokers Tell Their Tales," *Current Health 2*, November 1999, p. 16.

21. Quoted in Murphy, "Teen Smokers Tell Their Tales," p. 16.

22. Quoted in Bo Poertner, "Stores 'Stung' by Tobacco Sales to Minors," *Santa Ynez Valley (CA) News*, October 11, 2011. http://syvnews.com.

23. Quoted in Duff Wilson, "Senate Approves Tight Regulation over Cigarettes," *New York Times*, June 12, 2009, p. 1.

24. Matthew L. Myers, "FDA Rules Crack Down on Tobacco Marketing and Sales to Kids," news release, Campaign for Tobacco-Free Kids, March 18, 2010. www.tobaccofreekids.org.

25. Patrick Basham, "An Absence of Tobacco Evidence," Cato Institute, September 11, 2009. www.cato.org.

26. Allan M. Brandt, *The Cigarette Century: The Rise, Fall and Deadly Persistence of the Product That Defined America*. New York: Basic Books, 2007, pp. 386–387.

27. Quoted in Stuart Elliott, "Joe Camel, a Giant in Tobacco Marketing, Is Dead at 23," *New York Times*, July 11, 1997, p. D1.

28. Quoted in John Mintz and Saundra Torry, "Internal R.J. Reynolds Documents Detail Cigarette Marketing Aimed at Children," *Washington Post*, January 15, 1998, p. A1.

29. Quoted in Brian Hartman, "New Law Bans Flavored Cigarettes," ABC News, September 22, 2009. http://abcnews.go.com.

30. Quoted in Amy F. Bailey, Associated Press, "Officials Seek End to Flavored Cigarettes," *Dayton (OH) Daily News*, January 11, 2005.

31. Quoted in World Entertainment News Network, "Joosten Calls for *Mad Men* Smoking Disclaimer," October 6, 2010.

32. Janice Turner, "If You're Not Kate Moss, Smoking Isn't Cool," *Times* (London), March 12, 2011, p. 22.

33. Quoted in Mark Raymond, "Bill Would Raise Tobacco Age to 21," *Brown Daily Herald* (Providence, RI), April 6, 2010. www.browndailyherald.com.
34. Laurence Steinberg, "Raise Age to Buy Cigarettes to 21," CNN, April 18, 2011. http://articles.cnn.com.
35. Quoted in Raymond, "Bill Would Raise Tobacco Age to 21."

Chapter Three: Do Smoking Bans Violate the Rights of Smokers?

36. Quoted in Alex Rush, "Up in Smoke! Beach-Goers Protest the City's Ban on Smoking in Parks," *Brooklyn (NY) Paper*, June 1, 2011. www.brooklynpaper.com.
37. Quoted in Rosie Gray, "Audrey Silk, Smoker's Rights Advocate, Weighs In on Today's Smoking Ban Poll," *Village Voice*, August 8, 2011. http://blogs.villagevoice.com.
38. Quoted in Garth Johnston, "Audrey Silk, Smoker's Rights Activist," *Gothamist*, February 8, 2011. http://gothamist.com.
39. Quoted in Associated Press, "New York Court Upholds Firing Worker over Smoking Breaks," *Crain's New York Business*, August 8, 2008. www.crainsnewyork.com.
40. Quoted in Associated Press, "New York Court Upholds Firing Worker over Smoking Breaks."
41. Quoted in Joanne Deschenaux, "Is a 'Smoker-Free' Workplace Right for You?," *HR Magazine*, July 2011, p. 42.
42. Quoted in Ken Altucker, "Humana Won't Hire Smokers in Arizona," *USA Today*, July 1, 2011. www.usatoday.com.
43. Quoted in Jeremy W. Peters, "Company's Smoking Ban Means Off-Hours, Too," *New York Times*, February 8, 2005. www.nytimes.com.
44. Quoted in Peters, "Company's Smoking Ban Means Off-Hours, Too."
45. Quoted in Peters, "Company's Smoking Ban Means Off-Hours, Too."
46. Quoted in Deschenaux, "Is a 'Smoker-Free' Workplace Right For You?," p. 42.
47. Quoted in Deschenaux, "Is a 'Smoker-Free' Workplace Right For You?," p. 42.
48. American Civil Liberties Union, "Legislative Briefing Kit: Lifestyle Discrimination in the Workplace," December 31, 1998. www.aclu.org.
49. Radley Balko, "Those Who Take the Health Risks Ought to Pay," *Central New York Business Journal*, May 20, 2005, p. 25.

50. Quoted in Anemona Hartocollis, "Two Roll-Your-Own-Cigarette Stores to Close," *City Room* (blog), *New York Times*, December 21, 2011. http://cityroom.blogs.nytimes.com.

51. Quoted in Hartocollis, "Two Roll-Your-Own-Cigarette Stores to Close."

52. Quoted in Johnston, "Audrey Silk, Smoker's Rights Activist."

53. Samantha K. Graff, *There Is No Constitutional Right to Smoke*. St. Paul, MN: Tobacco Control Legal Consortium, 2008. http://publichealthlawcenter.org.

54. Graff, *There Is No Constitutional Right to Smoke*.

Chapter Four: Are There Other Ways to Get People to Stop Smoking?

55. Quoted in Maria Cheng and Toby Sterling, Associated Press, "Netherlands Backtracks on Antismoking Efforts," *Philadelphia Inquirer*, January 1, 2012, p. A12.

56. Quoted in Anna Holligan, "Dutch Unease over Cigarette Lobbying," BBC News, January 31, 2012. www.bbc.co.uk.

57. Quoted in William Estes, "VSC Tests Will Aim at Younger Smokers," *Los Angeles Times*, July 22, 1966, p. SF8.

58. Quoted in *New York Times*, "Teachers Urged Not to Smoke," February 19, 1965, p. A22.

59. Quoted in *USA Today*, "It Takes a Village to Quit," October 3, 2005, p. 1D.

60. Quoted in New York State Health Department, "State Health Department Unveils Hard-Hitting Smoking Cessation Public Service Announcements," news release, July 28, 2010. www.health.ny.gov.

61. Quoted in David Kesmodel and Betsy McKay, "Anti-smoking Programs Are Slashed," *Wall Street Journal*, November 9, 2010. http://online.wsj.com.

62. Quoted in American Lung Association, "The Year in Tobacco Control," January 19, 2012. www.lungusa.org.

63. Quoted in Tara Parker-Pope, "Safer Cigarettes: A History," *NOVA*, December 2, 2001. www.pbs.org.

64. Quoted in Parker-Pope, "Safer Cigarettes."

65. Quoted in Daily Beast, "Snuffed Out: Probing the Myth that 'Light' Cigarettes Are Better for You," November 19, 2007. www.thedailybeast.com.

66. Quoted in Duff Wilson, "FDA Seeks Explanation of Marlboro Marketing," *New York Times*, June 18, 2010, p. B6.

67. Quoted in CBS News, "Cigarette Packs Get Colorful for 'Light' Ban," June 4, 2010. www.cbsnews.com.
68. Quoted in ABC News, "How Safe Are E-cigarettes?," January 30, 2011. http://abcnews.go.com.
69. Quoted in Stacia Glenn, "Ruling OKs E-cigarette Use in Pierce County Bars, Workplaces," *Tacoma (WA) News Tribune*, June 2, 2011. www.thenewstribune.com.
70. Quoted in Glenn, "Ruling OKs E-Cigarette Use in Pierce County Bars, Workplaces."

Chapter Five: Would a Comprehensive Smoking Ban Be Effective?

71. Quoted in Christine Graf, "No Smoking, Please," *Faces*, March 2007, p. 32.
72. Quoted in Eric Weiner, "The First Non-smoking Nation," *Slate*, January 20, 2005. www.slate.com.
73. James Colgrove, Ronald Bayer, and Kathleen Bachynski, "Nowhere Left to Hide? The Banishment of Smoking from Public Places," *New England Journal of Medicine*, June 23, 2011, p. 2375.
74. Quoted in Bob Orr, "Cigarette Smuggling Costs States Billions," CBS News, October 18, 2011. www.cbsnews.com.
75. Quoted in Gary Fields, "States Go to War on Cigarette Smuggling," *Wall Street Journal*, July 20, 2009, p. A6.
76. Quoted in Peter Benson, *Tobacco Capitalism: Growers, Migrant Workers, and the Changing Face of a Global Industry*. Princeton, NJ: Princeton University Press, 2012, p. 102.
77. Quoted in Patrik Jonsson, "Along Tobacco Row, a Changed Culture," *Christian Science Monitor*, October 21, 2004, p. 1.
78. Quoted in Lauren Etter, "Nicotine Buzz: US Farmers Rediscover the Allure of Tobacco," *Wall Street Journal*, September 18, 2007, p. A1.
79. Quoted in MSNBC.com, "Economic Fears Are Snuffing Out Smoking Bans," February 4, 2009. www.msnbc.msn.com.
80. Quoted in NJ.com, "Atlantic City Reconsiders Casino Smoking Ban," September 29, 2009. www.nj.com.
81. Quoted in MSNBC.com, "Economic Fears Are Snuffing Out Smoking Bans."
82. Quoted in Lara Salahi, "FDA Appeals Block on Cigarette Warning Labels," ABC News, November 30, 2011. http://abcnews.go.com.
83. Quoted in Duff Wilson, "Court Blocks Graphic Labels on Cigarette Packs," *New York Times*, November 8, 2011, p. B2.

Related Organizations and Websites

American Cancer Society (ACS)

250 Williams St. NW
Atlanta, GA 30303
phone: (800) 227-2345
website: www.cancer.org

The ACS supports research and provides public education about the disease. Students who want to learn about lung cancer can follow the "Learn About Cancer" link on the organization's website to access the organization's *Tobacco-Related Cancers Fact Sheet.*

American Civil Liberties Union (ACLU)

125 Broad St., 18th Floor
New York, NY 10004
phone: (212) 549-2500
website: www.aclu.org

The ACLU has aided smokers, defending them against lifestyle discrimination laws in which employers mandate that workers cannot smoke on their own time. By following the link for "Workplace Privacy" on the ACLU's website, students can find news releases, position papers, and other resources on the rights of workers to smoke off the job.

American Legacy Foundation

1724 Massachusetts Ave. NW
Washington, DC 20036
phone: (202) 454-5555
website: www.legacyforhealth.org

Since 2000 the American Legacy Foundation has provided $150 million in grants to help finance antismoking campaigns. One project sponsored by the foundation studied the use of cigarettes in movies; visitors to the organization's website can access the report, *Trends in Top Box Office Movie Tobacco Use.*

American Lung Association (ALA)

1301 Pennsylvania Ave. NW, Suite 800
Washington, DC 20004
phone: (202) 785-3355
fax: (202) 452-1805
e-mail: info@lung.org
website: www.lung.org

The ALA sponsors research into lung disease and advocates against cigarette use. Visitors to the organization's website can access the annual report *State of Tobacco Control*, in which the ALA assesses efforts by the states to tax and regulate tobacco use.

Americans for Nonsmokers' Rights

2530 San Pablo Ave., Suite J
Berkeley, CA 94702
phone: (510) 841-3032
fax: (510) 841-3071
website: www.no-smoke.org

Americans for Nonsmokers' Rights lobbies for state and federal laws that limit access to cigarettes and to places where smoking is permitted. By following the link for "Target Populations," visitors to the organization's website can learn how the tobacco industry targets specific ethnic groups and how smoking and secondhand smoke affects those groups.

Campaign for Tobacco-Free Kids

1400 Eye St. NW, Suite 1200
Washington, DC 20005
phone: (202) 296-5469
fax: (202) 296-5427
website: www.tobaccofreekids.org

The group lobbies specifically for laws that restrict access of young people to tobacco. Students who visit the organization's website can access the *Tobacco Unfiltered* blog, in which news and commentary on antismoking developments are posted.

Centers for Disease Control and Prevention (CDC)

Office on Smoking and Health
4770 Buford Highway, MS K-50
Atlanta, GA 30341-3717
phone: (800) 232-4636
website: www.cdc.gov/tobacco

The CDC's Office on Smoking and Health coordinates the agency's research into the health effects of tobacco use. Visitors to the office's website can find data sheets providing facts on the economic impact of tobacco use, the health effects of smoking, the dangers of secondhand smoke, how smokeless tobacco can cause disease, and statistics on young smokers.

Illinois Smokers Rights

PO Box 408
Lake Bluff, IL 60044
e-mail: info@smokersclub.com
website: www.illinoissmokersrights.com

Illinois Smokers Rights is one of many organizations that have formed to oppose high taxes on cigarette sales and to otherwise defend the rights of smokers to enjoy cigarettes where they please. Visitors to the group's website can access the *United Pro-Choice Smokers Rights Newsletter*, in which many smokers post news of their movement.

New York City Citizens Lobbying Against Smoker Harassment (NYC CLASH)

PO Box 1036
Brooklyn, NY 11234
phone: (917) 888-9317
e-mail: nycclash@nycclash.com
website: www.nycclash.com

NYC CLASH is one of the most active smokers' rights groups in the country. Its founder, Audrey Silk, organizes rallies, grants media interviews, and testifies before city council meetings when antismoking measures are on the agenda.

Surgeon General

Tower Building
Plaza Level 1, Room 100
1101 Wooton Pkwy.
Rockville, MD 20852
phone: (240) 276-8853
fax: (240) 453-6141
website: www.surgeongeneral.gov

Since Surgeon General Luther Terry issued the first report linking smoking with disease in 1964, his successors in the office have released numerous other studies outlining the risks of smoking. Students who visit the surgeon general's website can access these reports by typing the word "smoking" into the site's search engine.

US Food and Drug Administration (FDA)

10903 New Hampshire Ave.
Silver Spring, MD 20993
phone: (888) 463-6332
website: www.fda.gov

Congress provided the FDA with wide-ranging powers to control the tobacco industry in 2009 when lawmakers adopted the Family Smoking Prevention and Tobacco Control Act. By following the link for "Tobacco Products" on the FDA's website, students can read the terms of the law and find updates on how the agency has implemented new regulations on tobacco use.

Additional Reading

Books

Peter Benson, *Tobacco Capitalism: Growers, Migrant Workers, and the Changing Face Of A Global Industry*. Princeton, NJ: Princeton University Press, 2012.

Rosemary Elliot, *Women and Smoking Since 1890*. Oxford, England: Routledge, 2011.

Barbara M. Hahn, *Making Tobacco Bright: Creating an American Commodity, 1617–1937*. Baltimore: Johns Hopkins University Press, 2011.

Siddhartha Mukherjee, *The Emperor of All Maladies: A Biography of Cancer*. New York: Scribner, 2010.

Robert N. Proctor, *Golden Holocaust: Origins of the Cigarette Catastrophe and the Case for Abolition*. Berkeley: University of California Press, 2012.

Periodicals

Sara Afzal, "Smokers Need Not Apply: Is Hiring Ban Trend of The Future?," *Christian Science Monitor*, November 17, 2010.

Maria Cheng and Toby Sterling, Associated Press, "Netherlands Backtracks on Antismoking Efforts," *Philadelphia Inquirer*, January 1, 2012.

James Colgrove, Ronald Bayer and Kathleen Bachynski, "Nowhere Left to Hide? The Banishment of Smoking from Public Places," *New England Journal of Medicine*, June 23, 2011.

Michael B. Siegel, "A Smoking Ban Too Far," *New York Times*, May 6, 2011.

Liz Szabo, "Study: Camel No. 9 Cigarette Ads Appeal to Teen Girls," *USA Today*, March 15, 2010.

Internet Sources

Centers for Disease Control and Prevention, "Economic Facts About U.S. Tobacco Production and Use." www.cdc.gov/tobacco/data_statistics/fact_sheets/economics/econ_facts.

National Cancer Institute, "Light Cigarettes and Cancer Risk." www.cancer.gov/cancertopics/factsheet/Tobacco/light-cigarettes.

PBS Kids, "Smoking: AnimAction," 2005. http://pbskids.org/itsmylife/body/smoking/article6.html.

Schaffer Library of Drug Policy, "History of Tobacco Regulation." www.druglibrary.org/schaffer/library/studies/nc/nc2b_10.htm.

Joy Johnson Wilson, "Summary of the Attorneys General Master Tobacco Settlement Agreement," University of Dayton, March 1999. http://academic.udayton.edu/health/syllabi/tobacco/summary.htm#Glance.

Index